Wiber

Geordi gripped the sides of his seat, holding on while the aquashuttle slammed into the sea floor again.

"When we stop moving, I'm going outside," Geordi said. "The grapples won't let go."

"That is dangerous undertaking," Yoshi replied. "I, too, will go. Perhaps with more muscle, job will be done quicker."

"Thanks, Yoshi." Geordi was surprised at how much better Yoshi's offer made him feel. Too many things could go wrong once he left the safety of the shuttle.

Geordi looked out the window. More chunks of debris sailed past them, but the shuttle appeared to be moving slower. He glanced down at the speed gauge, which confirmed his guess. "We're slowing down. Let's suit up so we'll be ready when we stop."

He unrolled his suit, admiring the lightweight, waterproof fabric. He smiled, thinking he would almost enjoy going outside wearing this suit. He glanced out the window and froze.

Two rock towers, fifty or sixty feet high and as many feet apart, loomed out of the darkness. The shuttle and the station were headed right for them. "Brace yourselves!" he yelled. "We're going to crash!"

D0028714

Star Trek: The Next Generation
STARFLEET ACADEMY

Star Trek: Deep Space Nine

Available from MINSTREL Books

STAR TREK
THE NEXT GENERATION®

STARFLEET ACADEMY™ #5

ATLANTIS STATION
V. E. Mitchell

Interior illustrations by
Todd Cameron Hamilton

A
MINSTREL®
BOOK

PUBLISHED BY POCKET BOOKS

New York   London   Toronto   Sydney   Tokyo   Singapore

A MINSTREL PAPERBACK *ORIGINAL*

A Minstrel Book published by
POCKET BOOKS, a division of Simon & Schuster Inc.
1230 Avenue of the Americas, New York, NY 10020

Copyright © 1994 by Paramount Pictures. All rights reserved.

STAR TREK is a Registered Trademark of
Paramount Pictures.

This book is published by Pocket Books, a division of
Simon & Schuster Inc., under exclusive license from
Paramount Pictures.

ISBN: 0-671-88449-2

First Minstrel Books printing August 1994

10 9 8 7 6 5 4 3 2 1

A MINSTREL BOOK and colophon are registered trademarks
of Simon & Schuster Inc.

Cover art by Catherine Huerta

Printed in the U.S.A.

To
all the Next Generation fans
who know *that*
Geordi is really the hero

STARFLEET TIMELINE

2264

The launch of Captain James T. Kirk's five-year mission, _U.S.S. Enterprise,_ NCC-1701.

2292

Alliance between the Klingon Empire and the Romulan Star Empire collapses.

2293

Colonel Worf, grandfather of Worf Rozhenko, defends Captain Kirk and Doctor McCoy at their trial for the murder of Klingon chancellor Gorkon.

Khitomer Peace Conference, Klingon Empire/Federation (_Star Trek VI_).

2323

Jean-Luc Picard enters Starfleet Academy's standard four-year program.

2328

The Cardassian Empire annexes the Bajoran homeworld.

2341

Data enters Starfleet Academy.

2342

Beverly Crusher (née Howard) enters Starfleet Academy Medical School, an eight-year program.

2346

Romulan massacre of Klingon outpost on Khitomer.

2351

In orbit around Bajor, the Cardassians construct a space station that they will later abandon.

2353

William T. Riker and Geordi La Forge enter Starfleet Academy.

2354

Deanna Troi enters Starfleet Academy.

2356

Tasha Yar enters Starfleet Academy.

2357

Worf Rozhenko enters Starfleet Academy.

2363

Captain Jean-Luc Picard assumes command of <u>U.S.S. Enterprise</u>, NCC-1701-D.

2367

Wesley Crusher enters Starfleet Academy.
An uneasy truce is signed between the Cardassians and the Federation.
Borg attack at Wolf 359; First Officer Lieutenant Commander Benjamin Sisko and his son, Jake, are among the survivors.
<u>U.S.S. Enterprise</u>-D defeats the Borg vessel in orbit around Earth.

2369

Commander Benjamin Sisko assumes command of Deep Space Nine in orbit over Bajor.

Source: <u>Star Trek</u>® <u>Chronology</u> / Michael Okuda and Denise Okuda

ATLANTIS STATION

CHAPTER

1

Geordi La Forge hurried along the corridor toward Starfleet Academy's shuttle pad. He wasn't quite running, because running would get him a lecture from any passing instructor or upperclassman, and then he would be *really* late—but he wasn't exactly walking, either. If only his Warp Dynamics class hadn't run overtime—*again*—he wouldn't be ten minutes late. It would be just like Lieutenant Muldov—the teacher who organized this field trip—to order the shuttle out on schedule.

Geordi groaned and increased his speed. He *had* to be on that shuttle. By the time he'd gotten around to signing up for the class field trip, there had been only three spaces left. Today was the one time when he didn't have a test in another class.

He should have signed up earlier, Geordi knew. Doing well in Lieutenant Muldov's Introduction to Planetary Exploration was mandatory for any cadet who wanted to get ahead in Starfleet. In fact, Geordi had heard it whispered, doing well in Exploration was more important than the legendary *Kobayashi Maru* test. After all, Starfleet had plenty of jobs for people who failed their command-officer testing, but there wasn't much one could do if one didn't know how to investigate strange environments.

It was just that Lieutenant Muldov's class wasn't his favorite. Perhaps because he saw things so much differently than everyone else, the class seemed almost irrelevant. Geordi couldn't remember when he *hadn't* felt like he was exploring an exotic world. Warp dynamics, on the other hand, was so alien, so much a world of the mind, that most of his classmates were more disadvantaged than Geordi. After the struggle to imagine the world around him before he got his VISOR, visualizing how a ship's warp drive affected the universe was a fascinating game.

The door leading to the landing pad whisked open. Geordi scanned the area with his VISOR. The VISOR, a Visual Instrument and Sensory Organ Replacement device, compensated for his blindness. The sensory imputs spotted the telltale heat sources that told him where his classmates were. He threaded his way through the shuttles until he reached the one assigned to his group. It was an aquashuttle, more compact and streamlined than the standard atmospheric craft.

"It is about time you got here." The open hostility in the soft, lisping voice made Geordi cringe. Ven of Almadixarian was an Andorian. He had blue skin and shoulder-length white hair. Small, curved antennae on the top of his head gave him extremely sensitive hearing. Like all his people, he was hot-tempered and quick in his judgments. Geordi didn't know how, but he had offended Ven on the first day of class. Their relationship had gotten worse as the semester progressed.

"He is twelve point three minutes late." T'Varien, the dark-haired Vulcan girl, deliberately ignored Geordi. Her upswept eyebrows lowered as she turned toward the shuttle's controls. "I shall note the reason for our deviation from the filed flight plan in the ship's log."

"I'm sorry I'm late." Geordi threw himself into the unoccupied seat, panting for breath. "Jes'NDau kept class late again."

"Honorable Jes'NDau never keeps our class over. It is most shameful to hide one's mistakes behind story of teacher's offenses." Yoshi Nakamura looked over his shoulder at Geordi, his expression as bland as T'Varien's. Yoshi was from a colony world settled by traditionalist Japanese, Geordi remembered. He seemed determined to make his classmates behave like sixteenth-century samurai. Worse still, he wouldn't believe anything that differed from his own experience.

Gritting his teeth to keep from arguing, Geordi buckled his safety harness. How had he gotten stuck on the same field trip as the three most obnoxious cadets in the class? He checked to see who else was in the shuttle.

Amray and Amril Stenarios sat in the rear seats. Both girls had dark eyes and dark, curly hair tied back in ponytails. Their identical, olive-skinned faces wore identical expressions of long-suffering patience. They were clones, two of six genetically identical girls. They usually stuck together and rarely had much to say. Geordi didn't think they could read each other's minds, but their team-

3

work was close enough to make some of his classmates wonder.

The other two cadets were Lissa Jordan and Todd Devereau. Geordi didn't know either of them very well. Lissa was tall and slender, with short copper-colored hair. Her huge, flashing smile always made Geordi's palms sweat; in fact, that happened even when she wasn't smiling at him.

Todd was shorter than Geordi and had blond hair and blue eyes. On the first day of class, he had announced that he was going to be Starfleet's finest captain, better even than the legendary James T. Kirk. Most of Geordi's friends laughed at Todd's claims, but Geordi didn't know Todd well enough to know if he could succeed.

The shuttle shivered as Ven brought the engines to full power. Geordi wiggled himself into a more comfortable position as Ven cleared the aquashuttle for launch. Within moments, they were airborne and on their way.

As the shuttle soared through the sky, Geordi took out his PADD to read his assignment. The class had been split into teams of eight. Each group, like a starship's away team, was given its "mission" as it left the Academy. After the field trip, each cadet would write a report, just as Starfleet officers did when they described what they found on new planets.

Geordi grinned as he read the words on his screen. His team was assigned to visit Research Station Atlantis. Two centuries earlier, volcanic eruptions had formed a new island in the middle of the Atlantic Ocean. It had been named Isla del Fuego, Island of Fire. To study the new island and the Mid-Atlantic Ridge near it, scientists had built Atlantis Station.

He continued reading. The main station, built on the island, had work space for fifty to seventy-five scientists. These people explored the island and its volcano, the ocean around it, and the nearby ocean floor.

For Geordi, the undersea dome was the most interesting part of the station. It was located almost two kilometers below the surface of the ocean. The thirty people assigned there lived and worked in the strangest and most dangerous place on Earth.

They were over halfway to the station before Geordi realized that Ven was still flying the shuttle. "We're supposed to trade off the pilot's duties." His voice was sharp with protest. According to the duty roster, Ven should have given him command of the shuttle fifteen minutes ago.

"I only fly with qualified pilots," Ven said in a tone that implied that only he was qualified. "The computer aboard this shuttle does not show a passing score on your flight tests."

"My scores are higher than yours, and you know it! I had the top qualifying scores on the navigation specialty test this year!" Learning to interpret the flight controls through his VISOR had *not* been easy. To earn his high scores, he had spent many extra hours practicing his piloting skills.

Geordi squeezed his fist against his leg. He had been looking forward to piloting a real shuttle instead of the Academy's training ships. Still, it wouldn't do to lose his temper, even if Ven had somehow deleted his flight rating from the shuttle's computer.

"We changed the piloting schedule before you arrived." T'Varien's tone was absolutely neutral. "It is illogical for you to assume that your tardiness will go unpunished."

That's not your job! Geordi caught himself before he said the words aloud. Arguing with them would not change their minds. All he could do was control his temper and excel on the rest of the assignment.

He began reading again. After losing points for not taking his turn as pilot, he needed much higher scores on everything else. He had his work cut out for him.

CHAPTER

Ven was still piloting the shuttle when they arrived at Isla del Fuego. Except for Geordi and the Stenarios clones, the other cadets had traded off the copilot's duties. Amril and Amray insisted on working as a team, but Ven refused to let anyone replace him as pilot. Geordi wondered how soon the shuttle's computer would grade the Andorian down for interfering with his classmates' work.

Despite Geordi's worries, Ven landed the shuttle like an experienced pilot. The door slid upward, letting a warm breeze into the cabin. Geordi took a deep breath. The air smelled of salt, seaweed, and a hint of sulfur. Eagerly, he unbuckled his safety harness and hurried outside.

The sunlight was so bright that it temporarily overloaded his VISOR. Everything was white, hot, too intense for him to sort out. The blazing light translated into fiery needles jabbing through his head.

"Quit blocking the door." Someone bumped Geordi from behind. He thought it was Ven, but the pain from the light made it hard to be sure. "If you cannot see what you are doing, get out of the way."

Someone else pushed past him on the other side. Geordi stumbled and lost his balance. He went down on his hands and knees. The crushed gravel of the landing field burned into his palms.

Before he could react, hands grasped his shoulders. "Are you all right?" The girl's voice was unfamiliar.

Struggling to get his bearings, Geordi straightened to a kneeling position. He wasn't hurt—at least, not seriously. One of his knees felt scraped, even through his uniform, but he wasn't going to admit that right now. If what had happened was an accident because everyone was too impatient to get outside, he didn't want to call any more attention to himself. His only real problem was the brilliant sunshine. Carefully, he adjusted the inputs from his VISOR, setting the sensitivity to a lower level.

The landing field was one of the few level areas on the island. To the north, the black mass of the volcano towered over them. Geordi's VISOR told him the summit was hotter than the rest of the mountain. He thought he saw steam rising from the volcano's mouth. In the opposite direction, foam-tipped waves rolled onto the beach.

"Are you all right?" the new girl asked again.

"Yeah. I'm fine." Geordi thought his voice sounded a little shaky. Luckily, no one else noticed. He stood quickly, before anyone decided to help him.

The girl stepped away and faced the group. She was short and had long, dark hair. Her skin was deeply tanned from spending long hours in the hot sun. Much to Geordi's surprise, she was wearing a Starfleet cadet's uniform.

"Welcome to Atlantis Station. I'm your guide, Leilani Kamehameha. I'm a science specialist at the Academy, and I was assigned here for my senior project." She started toward the cluster of low, tan buildings opposite the landing field. "You're very lucky to be visiting us just now. We're getting some very exciting results in our work."

Inside the station, everything was cool and dim. With a sigh of relief, Geordi readjusted the inputs from his VISOR. Even with the trouble the device sometimes gave him, working without all the information it showed him was harder still. He was used to the VISOR, and he needed it to see the world around him.

Geordi had been born blind, without optic nerves to carry information from his eyes to his brain. The scientists who designed his VISOR gave him the best vision they could create. The device scanned the electromagnetic spectrum from infrared through ultraviolet, reading a far wider range of frequencies than a normal person could. The VISOR fed that information directly into Geordi's brain. Sometimes, having to sort through the extra information gave him a headache, but he figured it was worth it. The VISOR showed him things about his world that no one else could see.

Leilani gave them a moment to look around. They were in a large entry hall with a high ceiling. Brightly colored posters and displays covered every inch of wall space. A scale model of the island filled the center of the room.

"This is our main display area," Leilani said. "The Isla del Fuego Visitors Center receives over fifty thousand visitors a year. Of course," she paused, smiling, "most of them don't get the tour you're about to get."

"They probably don't have to write a paper, either," Todd said to Lissa under his breath.

Leilani focused an even wider smile on Todd, and his cheeks grew hot from embarrassment. Todd hadn't intended his comment for anyone but Lissa. "Actually, many of them do. Most of our visitors are students on class field trips. Isla del Fuego provides a unique opportunity to study the formation of an island and to observe how plant and animal populations evolve over time. Students in geology, biology, botany, ecology, and oceanography all gain valuable insights from the work we do on Isla del Fuego."

She studied the group. "Does anyone have any questions?" When no one did, she continued, "In that case, I'll give you your communicators and we can begin your tour."

Leilani went to a console near the door. Geordi was the first person in line. She took a communicator from the drawer and touched it to a sensor pad. After telling the computer how long he would be on the island, she gave the communicator to him.

While he waited for the others, Geordi examined the model of the island. Isla del Fuego was a single volcano, a massive pile of rock built up from the ocean floor nearly three miles below. Most such volcanoes never reached sea level. Of those that did, many did not survive the ceaseless battering of the ocean's waves. Within a few years, the new islands were worn down below sea level and never seen again.

Against the odds, Isla del Fuego had grown into permanent land. The island had an oval shape, with the summit of the mountain to the west. The field where they had landed was the largest patch of level ground on the island, and most of Atlantis Station had been built in the area. A few structures were located elsewhere on the island.

The model was incredible. With all the details it showed, Geordi could have spent the rest of the day studying it. Suddenly he felt very small and unimportant. The universe held so many surprises and promised so many exciting adventures that he would need dozens of lifetimes to explore all the possibilities. How could he ever learn enough to get through his Academy classes and become a Starfleet officer?

Leilani stepped in front of the model. "Let me introduce you to Isla del Fuego, the Island of Fire. Most of you have seen our display. This is an accurate scale model of the island, showing every lava flow and volcanic vent. Our people work very hard to keep it up-to-date."

"How difficult can that be? Mountains aren't like cities. People don't rebuild them every week." Lissa's puzzled tone reminded Geordi that she came from Holloway Base. Built on an airless moon, the landscape outside the base's dome was sterile and unchanging.

Leilani explained, "Isla del Fuego is on the most active part of the Mid-Atlantic Ridge. The sea floor here spreads at the rate of two to three centimeters per year."

She paused, grinning. "That doesn't sound very fast,

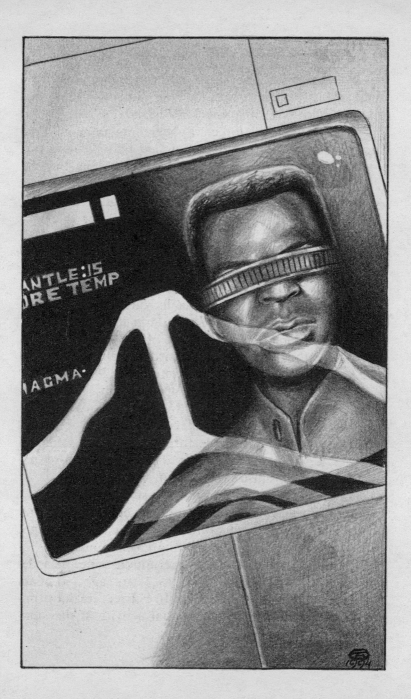

but it's enough. As the ridge pulls apart, hot rock from deep inside the earth fills the gap. Some of that rock piled up here until it formed this island."

"Anyone who has taken a beginning geology class knows that." T'Varien's tone implied that the information was so basic that every grade-school child knew it. *On Vulcan, they probably do,* Geordi thought. His sister Ariana had gone to school with a Vulcan girl for a while, and T'Loura had been several years younger than her classmates.

Leilani's face flushed with anger, but her voice remained calm. "That's true. However, people often have trouble connecting what they learn in class with the world around them. It's especially difficult in geology, where the things we study are so large."

T'Varien flipped her bangs out of her eyes. "Can we not assume that everyone has heard this elementary lecture and proceed to something interesting?"

Geordi tried to remember enough from his geology class to ask an intelligent question. While he was thinking, help came from an unexpected source.

"Please continue with lecture, Honorable Leilani," Yoshi said. "Humble students should show more patience in learning history of island."

" '*Honorable* Leilani'?" Todd whispered.

Geordi shrugged. Yoshi's manners were excessive, but he was glad no one else heard Todd. Finally, he thought of a question. "How often has the volcano erupted?"

"There have been ten major eruptions since Isla del Fuego rose from the ocean 215 years ago." Leilani flashed Geordi a grateful smile. "In between major eruptions, the volcano shows occasional activity at the sum-

14

mit. You're in luck. Two lava fountains started erupting last night."

"Will it be possible for us to see them?" Judging from Ven's tone, he really wanted to see the volcano erupt. That surprised Geordi. The Andorian didn't seem interested in the sciences. From what Geordi had seen, Ven preferred to order his classmates around. He clearly saw himself as a future starship captain. However, Geordi didn't want to serve under him. Ven was too sure of his own abilities and too quick to condemn others.

Leilani nodded yes to Ven's question. "We'll fly around the mountain and see the fire fountains. Before that, though, we'll tour the station's research labs. I think you'll enjoy seeing how we study the inside of the volcano."

With that, she started down the corridor. Geordi and his classmates fell in line behind her.

The deep imaging lab was an engineer's dream. The gleaming consoles, flashing monitors, and complex equipment begged for someone to put them through their paces. Geordi stood in the door admiring everything. He wished he had a week to learn how each device worked.

It wasn't the first time he'd had a clear picture of where he wanted to go in Starfleet. Like most cadets, Geordi was overwhelmed by the range of specialties Starfleet offered him. But he *knew* what he wanted—he wanted to be the person who made everything work.

Chief Engineer Geordi La Forge. Yes, it had a nice ring to it. Someday that was who he was going to be. However, he realized, someday was a long way off. At the moment, he'd better pass *this* class.

15

"And this screen tells us what's happening inside the volcano," Leilani was saying. "The colors show the temperature of the rocks below the surface."

Geordi moved closer to the monitor. It showed a cutaway view of the mountain. A vertical strip of bright yellow ran from the bottom of the screen to the mouth of the volcano. It could have been a picture straight from his geology text.

Leilani pointed to several consoles on the far wall. "The best way for you to understand this is to analyze the problem. These work stations receive data from our sensor arrays on the mountain.

"For the next hour, you will be a science team exploring a new planet. Your mission is to study this volcano and prepare a report for your captain. Each of you should prepare your own analysis in addition to the group report." Leilani grinned at them. "Good luck," she said as she left the room.

CHAPTER
3

It was almost too good to be true, Geordi thought as he slid into his seat. He had half an hour to collect information from the most advanced sensor array on Earth before the cadets would prepare the group report. With that much time, he should have no trouble writing an individual report that would make up the points he had lost earlier.

He began with the temperature data. Sensors reported how hot the rocks were, starting at the Earth's surface and going deep underground.

Geordi arranged his information into vertical slices through the volcano. Each showed patches of hotter rock near the surface. When he arranged the profiles into a three-dimensional grid, he found the column of molten rock that Leilani had showed them. However, his screen displayed more details.

Several fingers of molten rock poked from the center column in various directions. The two largest branches were near the top of the mountain. One seemed to be moving upward as he watched. Geordi rotated the picture, trying to decide if he was imagining the movement.

He was so busy that, at first, Geordi didn't realize his chair was shaking. When he looked around, he saw that both clones were holding onto the counter's edge. *An earthquake?* Geordi wondered, as the shaking stopped. He'd heard about them, but he'd never been in one.

Curious, he asked the computer for information about earthquakes and Isla del Fuego. It gave him three screens of topics to choose from. *Too much data,* he thought. Which information would let him predict what the volcano would do?

"Computer," he ordered, "display all earthquakes for the previous month, coded by intensity." A bright fuzzy patch of dots appeared on the screen. Most were yellow or white, but scattered dots of other colors showed the larger earthquakes. Geordi couldn't see any pattern.

"Computer, display earthquakes according to time and date. Compression factor, 1.5 million." The pixels of light blinked on and off in rapid succession. Geordi still couldn't see any pattern. The points were too random. "Computer, have the locations of the earthquakes changed during the last month?"

"Analysis shows a 1.735% upward drift. The level of uncertainty is 5%, and the correlation coefficients are highly variable."

Geordi nodded. Measuring precise locations through many kilometers of rock was still not an exact science. "Computer, overlay earthquake locations with heat distribution profile."

The picture formed on his screen. The earthquake data mapped out a circular area about two kilometers beneath the ocean's floor. Geordi's heat profiles stopped four kilometers above it. "Computer, extend heat flow data to ten kilometers depth."

The central column extended downward. When it reached the earthquake zone, the bright yellow stripe expanded into a large bubble. Most of the earthquakes were taking place around its edges.

What do they called that? Geordi frowned, trying to remember. *Magma chamber?* Yes, that's what the geologists called that feature. Magma was their word for molten rock beneath the Earth's surface. A magma chamber was where the liquid rock collected. Motions in the molten rock often caused earthquakes in the solid rock around the magma chamber.

Could the volcano on Isla del Fuego be getting ready to erupt? Geordi wondered. What information would help him predict what would happen? The computer listed magnetic surveys, electrical surveys, records of how much the mountain was tilting, and chemical analyses of the gases being released from the volcano.

It was far too much information for one person to analyze in the time he had. With a slow grin, Geordi realized the reason for this exercise. With limited time for any mission, everyone had to work together to complete an assignment. Here they were doing the same project. However, on a normal mission, each person would study one aspect of the problem—one person observing the volcano, another collecting plant specimens, a third looking for sea life. Teamwork would give them more data than any single person could collect.

"It is now time for us to prepare our group report," T'Varien announced. She was acting as chief scientist for the exercise. Stopping beside Geordi, she looked at the information on his screen. "You have a great deal of data here, but it is meaningless without informed interpretations."

Geordi clenched his hand. Responding to the criticism would only get him into trouble. "It looks like the volcano is getting ready to erupt. With more time, I could predict when."

"Leilani already told us there were fire fountains on the summit." T'Varien's tone made Geordi feel like a four-year-old, and not a very smart one at that. "Why do you think your data shows anything more will happen?"

Geordi repeated her question to himself. Why *did* he think the volcano was going to erupt "soon"? His evidence wasn't conclusive, and "soon," in geological terms, might not be for fifty years. Still, there was something he couldn't quite spot, even with the extra powers of his VISOR. Some piece of evidence was teasing him for attention. He frowned, remembering how hot the top of the mountain had looked when they landed. Was that what was bothering him?

T'Varien moved on to the Stenarios clones. "You forgot to check how the temperature profiles vary over time," she told Amray. "If you had, you would know that these results are worthless."

"My screen shows that information," Amril said.

"It made more sense to create the profiles on my screen—" Amray said. Her olive-skinned finger traced the curves on the display.

"—while we ran the analyses on my machine," Amril continued, finishing her sister's sentence without missing a beat. She pointed to the matching curves on her screen.

"We agree with Cadet La Forge's suggestion—"

"—that the volcano will erupt soon."

"Perhaps within the next two weeks."

"That is absolute nonsense." Ven joined the argument, his antennae quivering with irritation. "The Academy would never send us on this trip if there was the slightest danger of an eruption."

Geordi frowned, looking for the flaw in Ven's logic. "Why wouldn't they send us anyway? *Especially* if they knew something unusual might happen. I mean, when we're officers, we'll have to deal with the unexpected all the time."

"And, of course, someone who cannot deal with the *expected* and make it to our shuttle on time can be trusted to deal with the unexpected." Ven's soft, hissing voice made his words sound even more threatening. "If you want an excuse to return to the Academy, I am sure the mail shuttle can take you back to dry land."

"I wasn't looking for an excuse to get out of the trip." From the look on Ven's face, Geordi didn't think the Andorian believed him. He turned back to his screen, fighting to keep from continuing the argument.

"All natural phenomena show wide random variations. It is normal for this volcano to occasionally display readings similar to the ones the sensors are reporting. Does anyone else disagree with the contents of our final report?" T'Varien asked. "Or does everyone understand the error the—other—members of the class made when they assumed high readings meant the volcano was about to erupt?"

Who gave you permission to ignore us? Geordi thought. He glanced toward the clones, but both Amril and Amray were staring at their displays. Amril was drumming her fingers on the control pad, her dark eyes filled with doubt. Amray was as rigid as a pillar of rock.

Amril was thinking about changing her report to match T'Varien's conclusions, Geordi realized. It would look strange if they signed their names to the group's report, saying the volcano was behaving normally, but turned in individual reports that reached the opposite conclusion. Lieutenant Muldov would certainly question their work.

Geordi reached for his control pad, then dropped his hand to his lap. "No," he whispered. "I know I'm right." A fair group report should reflect the work of each team member. The least he could do was be honest and turn in the work he had done.

"She shouldn't have dismissed our work. This type of problem—" Amril whispered to him.

Amray nodded and finished Amril's thought. "—has too many variables for anyone to be absolutely sure of the answers."

Geordi grinned at them, glad for their support. Even so, he was relieved when Leilani returned. He logged his work into the main computer and left the lab. With the report on file, he wouldn't be tempted to give in to group pressure and change it later.

CHAPTER 4

Outside, an airbus was waiting for them. On its side was a bright red logo—the outline of a volcano with the words "Isla del Fuego" in a circle around it. The cadets climbed into the bus and found seats.

Geordi sat in the front, behind Leilani. A glance at the controls told him that the trip was directed by the computer. The guide could pause the program to let them spend more time somewhere. Beyond that, they would see the same sights as every other visitor to the island.

Disappointed, Geordi fastened his safety harness. He wasn't sure what he'd expected, but he wanted their visit to the volcano to be special. Knowing they were getting a standard tour was a letdown.

He looked out the window, adjusting his VISOR to allow for the bright sun. The blocky, angular ends of the lava flows took on sharp edges and deep shadows. The sunlit surfaces read over fifty degrees hotter than the deep cracks between the boulders.

Leilani tapped the control pad and the bus shivered to life. It rose into the air, circling the station. They turned, heading up the mountain. Leilani pointed toward the jagged boulders that Geordi had been looking at.

"The rough, blocky rock you see is called *aa*. That's a Hawaiian word. It's spelled with two *a*'s, and you say both of them. Ah-ah." She gave them a well-timed grin. "That's the only easy thing about this stuff."

"It looks just like the rocks back home," Lissa said. "Can't you boulder-surf those hills?"

Leilani shook her head. "The gravity here on Earth is over ten times what it is on Holloway Base. When you jump, you don't move nearly as far."

T'Varien looked toward Lissa. "The rocks will pick up speed much faster than you are used to. If you do not keep out of the way, they will run you down."

"That's a good point," Leilani said. "Every time you go to a new environment, things change. Even the most basic things, like how high you can jump or how fast a rock will roll down a hill. New places are dangerous when you assume they are like places you already know."

Geordi gazed at the broken-up rocks and reflected on what a good point Leilani had made. If you lived long enough on a planet, you quit thinking about the gravity, and how long the days were, and how hot the summer was. Sometimes it wasn't easy to adjust to the changes. Both his parents were in Starfleet, and he'd moved around a lot when he was a kid. He'd never gotten used to some of the places they'd lived.

The airbus moved farther up the mountain. The rocks below them became smoother, with a twisted, ropelike

24

surface. "The rocks you are looking at now are *pahoehoe* basalt. Pa-ho-ee-ho-ee"—Leilani said the word slowly and clearly so they could all understand it—"is another Hawaiian word. We Hawaiians have always studied volcanoes with great interest."

Several of the cadets laughed. Lissa looked puzzled, not understanding the joke. Geordi decided she must not have taken any geology at the Academy. His teacher had talked about the Hawaiian volcanoes for a week. Some classes, he'd heard, spent even more time studying Hawaii.

They continued upward. Leilani talked most of the time. She pointed out the different lava flows, described each one, and gave the history of its eruption.

The mountainside was black and empty. From a distance, the rock looked like black syrup frozen into ropes and mounds and rivers. Most areas below were lifeless. In a few places, small, scraggly plants sprouted from cracks in the rocks.

"We're studying how plants grow on new rock," Leilani said. "The wind blows fine dust onto the island, and it's trapped in the rocks. Some plants appear within fifty years of an eruption."

"Where do the seeds come from?" Amray asked. Her face was pressed against the window.

"There weren't any plants here when the island formed." Amril leaned against her window in an identical position.

"The seeds were brought here by birds. They eat the berries for food, but they can't digest the seeds." Leilani gave the computer an order and they swung in a wide arc. A small valley filled with brush appeared beneath them. Geordi's VISOR picked out a dozen varieties of flora by how the light was reflected off the leaves. The pattern of the plants and rocks looked like a crazy quilt.

"Even now, we discover at least one new variety every year," Leilani continued. "As the plants break down the rocks to form soil, it becomes easier for more plants to grow."

They flew past the valley and continued up the mountain. The next valley appeared hotter to Geordi. He tried to check the different ranges from his VISOR, but the heat reflected from the black rocks looked very much like heat coming from beneath the surface.

Before he could decide which was which, they were over the next ridge and heading for the summit. The last slope was the steepest. The whine from the engines rose to a shrill pitch as the bus climbed the last few meters.

The ground flattened at the top. The bus landed a safe distance from the crater. A cloud of steam rose ahead of them. The ground was covered with small reddish chunks of rock.

The door opened, letting in a blast of air that smelled of rotten eggs. "What's that horrid smell?" Lissa asked, scowling.

"That smell is sulfur from the volcano," T'Varien said. She moved quickly for the door, with Ven close behind her. By the time Geordi got outside, both were looking over the edge. They were arguing about the best way to reach the floor of the crater.

"You will *not* go down there!" Leilani's voice cracked like a whip. *"No one* goes down there without proper equipment. And that's *after* they get permission from the director."

The rocks crunched beneath Geordi's boots. He bent down and picked up one. It was a couple of centimeters in diameter and full of holes.

"We wish to study the volcano to the best of our ability." T'Varien's tone sounded reasonable. "We must get closer to do this. You are keeping us from doing our assignment."

Geordi rolled the piece of rock in his hand. The sharp edges cut into his hand like glass. When he looked closer, he saw that it *was* glass. A thin coating of iron oxide, much like rust, covered the unbroken surfaces.

"No." Leilani stood her ground, acting as though she dealt with unreasonable cadets every day. "Anyone who steps over that edge will be expelled from Starfleet Academy immediately."

Geordi hurried forward, curious to see why his classmates were so eager to climb into the crater. More rocks crunched under his boots and scattered ahead of him. A gust of hot, sulfur-laden air hit him as he reached the top.

At his feet, the ground dropped away. Sheer cliffs surrounded the bowl-shaped crater. Three fire fountains, one more than they had been told, played near the opposite wall. The crater's floor was almost two hundred meters below. Startled, Geordi stepped back.

"True samurai must never show sign of fear." Yoshi moved to the crater's edge. "Force of nature is not dangerous like honorable opponent in battle."

"Tell that to the people who get killed in natural disasters," Geordi muttered. Try as they might, scientists still couldn't predict every major earthquake or hurricane or flood. Each year, people were killed because they ignored the warnings or because they weren't warned in time.

Geordi decided to play it safe. He could see well enough from where he was. Each fire fountain was throwing molten rock—it was called lava, he reminded himself—almost as high as the rim of the crater. The streams of lava looked like water squirted from a hose. At the base of each fountain, the lava was bright red, but it turned black as it cooled.

The drops of rapidly cooling rock crashed and tinkled on the ground like china plates dropped onto the floor. Larger blobs of still-molten lava made dull plops when they landed. Geordi wiped the sweat from his forehead. It was hard to believe it was so hot this far from the eruption.

"You are interfering with my right to practice my religion," Ven said. He was shouting to be heard over the clattering rocks. "The Observance of the Flames is central to all five major Andorian religions."

Wondering what would happen next, Geordi looked away from the fire fountains. Ven and T'Varien had split, with one on either side of Leilani.

"First, religious ceremonies on Isla del Fuego are restricted by the research station's charter. You must have permission from the director." Leilani crossed her arms over her chest and stared at Ven.

The Andorian flushed a darker shade of blue. "I protest most strongly. I have the right under the Federation charter to practice my religion."

"Granted." Leilani's face relaxed into an I've-got-you grin. Her teeth flashed against her tanned skin. "However, you're also a Starfleet cadet on an Academy assignment. As such, you can be dismissed from the Academy if you ignore my orders."

A tremor shook the mountain. Geordi felt the ground tilting beneath his feet. Rocks broke loose and fell into the crater. They clattered all the way down.

Another tremor hit, and Geordi felt himself skating toward the cliff. Something moved off to one side. He looked that way and saw Yoshi sliding over the edge.

Geordi threw himself flat and dug his toes into the loose rock. He reached for Yoshi, barely catching his hand. Yoshi's body swung into the cliff. The impact twisted Geordi's shoulder and jerked him toward the edge.

Digging his toes farther into the loose rock, Geordi brought his other hand forward to grab Yoshi. The weight dragged him closer to the edge. The rocks beneath him vibrated with an ominous cracking. "Hurry! It's giving way."

Yoshi struggled, his body swinging like a pendulum. Geordi pressed himself harder against the ground, but he kept sliding. His hands hung over empty air, then his arms followed.

Just as he knew he was going to fall, Geordi felt strong hands around his ankle. Moments later, another pair of hands grabbed his other ankle. He risked a glance over his shoulder. Leilani and T'Varien were holding his feet. They pulled, dragging him backward inch by inch.

He tightened his grip on Yoshi, hoping he could hang on until they were both safe. The rough pebbles cut into him, scraping his skin. The cracking sounds became louder.

Yoshi's head appeared above the cliff. The girls jerked

on Geordi's legs and Yoshi popped over the edge. Leilani and T'Varien dropped Geordi's ankles.

"Run!" Leilani ordered. She and T'Varien dashed for the airbus.

The ground shook harder. Geordi rolled over and got to his knees. Behind him, he heard the scatter of pebbles as Yoshi scrambled to his feet. The ground heaved drunkenly beneath him.

Geordi didn't bother to stand. Pushing off like a sprinter coming off the starting blocks, he lit out for the airbus. Yoshi was two steps behind him.

They threw themselves through the door. As Geordi stumbled to his seat, Leilani ordered an emergency lift-off. The bus jumped into the air, shoving him deep into the padding.

Beneath them, the side of the mountain crumbled and slid into the crater. Even through the walls of the airbus, the grinding and banging of the moving rocks were deafening. Clouds of dust made it impossible to see anything.

Geordi shivered, thinking how close they had come to being buried beneath the rockslide. From the silence in the bus, he decided his classmates were also shaken by the close call. He tightened his safety harness. For the moment, he was content to let the computer fly them back to the research station.

Back at the station, Leilani showed Geordi and his classmates to the cafeteria. He didn't notice until they were eating that she had left the room.

Geordi nibbled on his sandwich. He knew he should eat it, but he wasn't hungry. His narrow escape had shaken him more than he wanted to admit. He studied his classmates, comparing their actions with what his VISOR told him.

Ven was angry, and Geordi guessed he was still upset about not being allowed into the crater. The Stenarios clones were withdrawn, locked in their own world. Geordi saw the sideways looks and the small signals they gave each other, but he didn't know what they meant. T'Varien appeared calm, but Geordi's VISOR told him that her body temperature was down, a sure sign of stress. Yoshi also pretended that nothing was wrong, but his hands were shaking.

Lissa and Todd had been farthest from the crater, and Geordi couldn't tell how the experience had affected them. They were talking to each other in low tones, too softly for Geordi to hear. With a shrug, he turned his attention back to his sandwich.

Finally Yoshi spoke, giving Geordi a deep bow from the waist. "One must thank honorable classmate Geordi for saving worthless life. Deepest gratitude is humbly expressed."

"Uh—you're welcome, Yoshi." Geordi swallowed. "But I didn't do it alone. Leilani and T'Varien had to pull me out, or we both would have fallen."

Yoshi turned to T'Varien and gave her a deep bow. "Deepest gratitude is also extended to honorable class-mate T'Varien for assistance in rescue."

T'Varien raised one eyebrow. For a moment, Geordi was afraid she would give them a lecture on human failings. Instead, she nodded. "It is only logical to save the lives of one's crewmates. Starfleet does not approve of needless loss of life among its trained officers."

Suddenly, Geordi felt a lot better. T'Varien's lack of

feeling should have been depressing, but it had the opposite effect. *Maybe because that's what you expect her to
say,* he thought. Maybe he was beginning to understand her.

Whatever the reason, he was suddenly hungry. He pol-
ished off his sandwich and went back for another. Leilani
returned while he was finishing his cookies.

She pulled a chair up to the end of the table and sat,
facing them. "I have been talking with the director about
what happened this morning. You're all aware that every
Starfleet assignment is a journey into the unknown. None
of us knows when we may have a brush with death such
as we did this morning."

Leilani paused, waiting for her words to sink in.
Geordi thought she looked tired, as if the morning's ex-
citement had taken more out of her than it had from
the rest of them. "The director talked with your teacher
a few minutes ago. Lieutenant Muldov insisted that you
should continue your tour. He said that, on a real mission, no Starfleet officer has the option of giving up when
things become a little dangerous."

She drew in a deep breath, as though trying to steady
herself. *Why is she so tense?* Geordi wondered. Lieutenant Muldov's reaction was exactly what he had expected.
In a moment, he heard the answer.

"The director, however, feels you should be given the
option to finish this trip later. In principle, she agrees
that a real mission must continue. However, this morning
you saw more danger than many Starfleet officers meet
in a full tour of duty. It's unfair to treat such an experience as a routine training assignment."

Todd straightened in his chair. "If Lieutenant Muldov

33

says we should finish the trip, what's the problem? What are we waiting for?"

Leilani looked at each of them, paused for a moment, and then went on. She reached Geordi and stopped, studying his face. He read the question from her expression. Did he feel like continuing? He thought for a moment, then nodded. "We're here and it seems like it would be easier to finish the tour now. I think it might be harder to come back later."

The others nodded in agreement. T'Varien summed up their feelings best. "If we are to become Starfleet officers, we must act like Starfleet officers. It is illogical for us to expect easier treatment as cadets than we will receive as officers."

That doesn't mean we can't be nervous, Geordi thought. After this morning, he would see routine assignments in a much different light. When mountains crumbled beneath your feet, nothing in the universe was completely certain.

He was still thinking about that fifteen minutes later when they headed back for the aquashuttle. Even so, what else could go wrong? They had used a year's supply of bad luck that morning. This afternoon, everything would be just fine.

CHAPTER

To no one's surprise, Ven took the pilot's seat when the cadets boarded the aquashuttle. Geordi paused in the door, thinking how much he needed the points for piloting the ship. Ven had no right to keep him from doing that part of his assignment.

After this morning's close escape, though, the other cadets would support Ven. Geordi knew he could fly the shuttle, but the others would think he was still too rattled. He would be better off waiting until they left the lower station before he asked for his turn. That decided, Geordi headed aft, choosing the seat beside the rear viewport. Amril and Amray were in the seats ahead of him, while Todd and Lissa were on the other side of the aisle.

To Geordi's surprise, Leilani took the copilot's seat. T'Varien came aft, leaving Yoshi in the fold-out seat behind the flight officers. After watching T'Varien's stiff movements, Geordi concentrated on his PADD. The

Vulcan clearly believed she was a better copilot than Leilani.

"Prepare for departure," Leilani said. Geordi checked the buckle on his harness to make sure it was secure.

Ven wasted no time in taking the shuttle up. He made a full power lift-off that drove Geordi deep in his seat. The shuttle's nose pitched sharply upward, and Geordi felt like he was sitting on the side of a steep mountain.

They reached the top of their arc. Ven tipped the shuttle downward, pointing it toward the ocean's surface. In the brief moment before the computer adjusted for the change, they were in free fall. Geordi felt his stomach lurch and he fought to keep his lunch down.

"Do you *have* to be so dramatic?" Lissa asked. She looked pale and Geordi guessed her stomach felt like his.

"I calculated this as the optimum course for entering the ocean," Ven said without taking his eyes off the controls. The shuttle's engines whined as Ven increased power.

Geordi shook his head, not bothering to say anything. He'd calculated this problem a dozen ways, and Ven's solution wasn't close to the best answer. The Andorian was hotdogging, showing off to impress Leilani. Considering how the computer graded their piloting, it was a foolish thing to do. A routine dive would score far higher.

Fountains of spray erupted as the shuttle's nose hit the water. The entry was smooth. The aquashuttle slowed quickly as it switched to underwater-operations mode. Gaudy fish and floating seaweed flashed past the viewport, but they were gone almost as soon as Geordi spotted them. A glance around the cabin showed him that his classmates were as fascinated with the underwater view as he was.

Within seconds, they were below the photic zone, the layer of the ocean that the sun's light could penetrate. Blackness, permanent night, closed around the aquashuttle. Geordi shivered. The water outside was barely above freezing. The deeper they went and the closer they got to the lower station, the more icy water there was above them. If anything went wrong, they were a long way from safety.

He shivered again, thinking how like—yet how unlike—the deep oceans and outer space were. Both were dark. Space filled the universe with an infinite night speckled with stardust, but the black water outside his viewport could not have been more featureless if he had removed his VISOR.

Both were cold, although the emptiness of space was colder. And neither place contained air that humanoids could breathe. The vacuum of space could suck the air from an unprotected person's lungs as quickly as the crushing pressure of the deep oceans could force the water in.

He touched his waist pouch, reassuring himself that his rebreather was there. In an emergency, the unit would provide him with breathable air for several hours. *I hope the batteries are fully charged,* he thought. He also hoped he wouldn't need to use the device.

A faint green light flickered outside the window, then disappeared behind them. For a moment, Geordi thought he had imagined it.

"A phosphorescent fish!" Lissa pointed out the window. "Did you see it, Todd?"

Todd leaned across her, trying to see out the window. The absolute blackness had returned. "It's gone," he said, settling back into his seat. "They aren't usually found around here."

"That species does not favor habitats this near to the surface," T'Varien said. "There is too much competition for food."

"I suppose you know *exactly* which type of fish that was." Todd glared at the Vulcan. "Even if *you* didn't see it, either."

"My files list twenty-five species of phosphorescent fish that are sometimes found in life zones similar to the one we are passing through. Of those twenty-five, probabilities favor—"

"You mean, you're guessing." Todd laughed, a sound that held very little humor. "I can do that, too."

Blood rushed to T'Varien's face. Geordi didn't think the others could tell that she experienced any emotions, but his VISOR showed him the heat that surged to her face.

"That confirms our theory." Amray gave her clone sister a significant look.

Amril nodded. "The impending eruption is causing the deep-water organisms to abandon their habitats."

"There is a 1.5% chance that, at any given time, organisms from a deeper life zone will be found in shallower water." T'Varien's hand tightened around her PADD.

"The life zones in this area are deeper because of the warm surface temperatures." Amray acted like she hadn't heard T'Varien, although her words contradicted the Vulcan's statement.

"That variety of fish normally lives below the level of the lower station," Amril added.

"If this shuttle had the proper sensors, we could monitor the migrations—" Amray glanced toward the front of the shuttle. Ven's antennae were swiveled as far forward as he could get them.

The Andorian was trying to ignore the conversation, Geordi decided. Clearly he still didn't want to hear any suggestion that the volcano might erupt. That Leilani didn't say anything either must mean that the shuttle wasn't equipped with the special sensors needed for detailed underwater research.

"—and chart the movements to show when the volcano will explode." Amril finished her sister's sentence, matching tone and meter perfectly.

T'Varien turned toward the clones. Her Vulcan mask was firmly in place. "You do not have sufficient information to support your conclusions. It is not logical for you to continue to ignore that fact."

Amril and Amray looked at each other, then began giggling. Amray tried to say something and both girls laughed harder. Soon tears were streaming down their cheeks. "Not—" Amray said, gasping for breath between her giggles.

"—logical." Amril wrapped her arms around her stomach. Both girls howled even louder.

"I fail to see the humor in this situation." T'Varien looked from Amril to Amray. One of her eyebrows had disappeared into her bangs.

The giggling died down, replaced by Amril's and Amray's gasps for breath. Finally, both were able to talk.

Amray tugged her hand through her dark ponytail.

"It's not logical for us to believe that the volcano is going to erupt—"

"—because you disagree with our analysis. But the same reasoning makes it—"

"—equally illogical for you to believe an analysis—"

"—that neither of us supports."

"My analysis is based purely on logic." T'Varien's face was a rigid mask. "Each of the factors that are used to predict eruptions is within the normal range. If the volcano is behaving normally, it will not erupt."

Geordi frowned, trying to find the flaw in T'Varien's argument. Volcanoes were formed by eruptions. That meant eruptions were as "normal" as the quiet periods between them.

Amril shook her head impatiently. "We agree that each individual reading falls within the normal range—"

"—for the periods between eruptions. But *every* reading for *every* instrument is on the *high* end of the range. Everything suggests—"

The two girls glanced at each other and finished the sentence in unison. "—that the volcano is getting ready to blow up *big time.*"

T'Varien lifted one eyebrow. "Your conclusion is totally illogical. The sum cannot be greater than the numbers added to obtain it."

Geordi called up his report. Comparing his data with the historical records, he was surprised to find that T'Varien was right. Each of the present readings was matched by similar readings taken when the volcano had *not* erupted.

With nothing else to do until they got to the lower station, Geordi began cross-checking the data. The research was so absorbing that he lost track of everything but what he was reading on his PADD. His classmates' conversations and the thrum of the engines faded into the background.

Within ten minutes, he was more convinced than ever that he was right about a pending eruption. To prove it, he would need to check every record in the computer. However, the pattern he found was consistent. When only one type of sensor reading was high, nothing happened. When *all* the readings were high, the volcano erupted.

It wasn't a question of *if* the volcano was going to erupt, he realized. It was a question of *when*.

He leaned back in his seat, thinking. He was just a first-year cadet, and not even a science specialist. There were seventy-five professional scientists working on Isla del Fuego. Most of them knew more about the volcano than he did. If the pattern he had found was real, they should have noticed it.

Was the pattern real? *Yes,* Geordi decided. He was convinced that the volcano was going to erupt soon. However, in geologic terms, "soon" was a tricky word. For a planet, time was measured in thousands or millions of years. "Soon" could be five minutes—or five decades—from now.

"Leilani, do the geologists know when the volcano is going to erupt?" he asked.

She looked over her shoulder at him. "That's a major topic of research here. Isla del Fuego is not as predictable as the Hawaiian volcanoes. Our geologists think their models are accurate to within a day, but we haven't

41

had an eruption in twenty years. It's hard to check their predictions without any data."

"Thanks." Suddenly, Geordi felt much better. Even if the volcano was going to erupt, he didn't need to worry about it ruining their field trip. The experts had spent years studying the volcano. They would have ordered the cadets back to the Academy if they thought something would happen this afternoon.

Even so, Geordi was glad when he saw the first soft glow from the lower station's marker beacons. Sitting gave him too much time to think—and to worry. The lower station was a superb example of Federation engineering. He couldn't wait to explore it.

CHAPTER

The glow from the beacon grew brighter. Leilani turned to Ven. "I'm taking over."

"I am in command of this vessel," the Andorian replied. "I refuse to let an unqualified person endanger our lives."

"Exactly." Leilani gave him a tight smile. "You've never docked a shuttle underwater. Not even in the simulator."

Geordi grinned. It was good to see someone stand up to Ven. Underwater dockings weren't as easy as they looked. He'd practiced in the simulator, but had missed more times than he had succeeded. Luckily, Leilani had checked Ven's practice log.

Ven turned to his classmates for support. Geordi quickly looked out the window. He didn't want an inexperienced pilot trying to dock the aquashuttle. No one else stood up for Ven, either.

When he realized his classmates weren't going to help

him, Ven switched his controls to standby and took over the copilot's duties. Leilani brought her command functions on-line. "Cadet Ven, read off the approach distances," she ordered.

"Two hundred meters," Ven read from the screen. "One hundred fifty meters, one hundred twenty-five, one hundred."

Leilani reduced the power to the engines. Friction from the water slowed the shuttle faster than Geordi expected. Piloting underwater was more complicated than flying in the air or in space. Geordi remembered why he had found the underwater simulator sessions so difficult.

Ven continued to read off the distances, freeing Leilani to adjust for the unpredictable crosscurrents near the station. The computer could have reported the numbers. Having Ven read them showed him that the underwater approach wasn't as simple as he had assumed.

The shuttle coasted alongside the station. The rectangular airlock, surrounded by bright beacons, jutted out from the dome's smooth surface. Leilani tapped the port thrusters. The shuttle scooted sideways and bumped against the magnetic grapples with just enough force to engage the clamps and the airlock's seals.

A low, mechanical throbbing shook the shuttle, followed by the splash and slosh of water outside the door. Fascinated, Geordi listened as the water splashed lower and lower on the door.

"Does it always take this long?" Lissa's freckles stood out against her pale skin. She ruffled a hand through her coppery hair. Geordi tried to decide whether she had asked the question from impatience or from nerves.

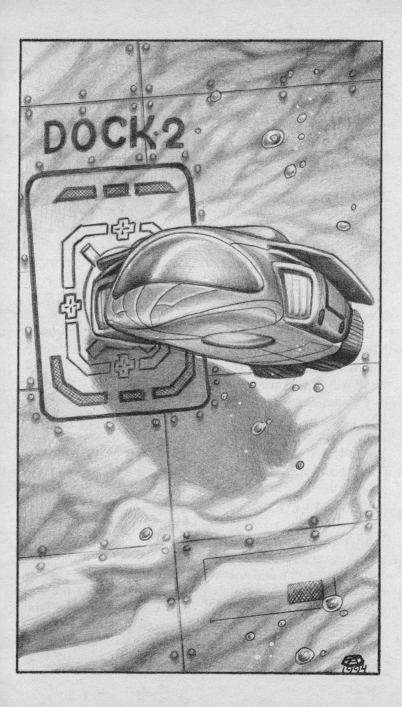

"This model of pump drains the water in the airlock while simultaneously adjusting the air pressure in the shuttle to match that of the station. Shortly our ears will—I believe the expression is—'pop.'" T'Varien's voice sounded strained. In a way, Geordi understood her reaction. Vulcan was a desert planet and it had no deep ocean research posts like Atlantis Station.

Geordi touched his rebreather again to remind himself that they *did* have backup systems for emergencies. As he did, he wondered why he felt so uneasy. He had spent most of his life on Starfleet vessels or on space stations, following his parents from one assignment to another. If something went wrong in deep space, rescue was a lot farther away than it was here.

Besides, he told himself, *nothing can possibly go wrong.* The lower dome of Atlantis Station was built to survive in its environment. They were as safe here as they would be on the island above.

Finally, the pumps finished draining the airlock. At the same time Geordi's ears popped. Around him the other cadets swallowed to adjust the pressure in their ears. The shuttle's door slid open, letting in a gust of damp, cold air. It smelled of iodine and scorched lubricant. Mixed with that was the flat, faintly metallic odor of air held too long in storage tanks.

The inner door slid open, letting them into the station. The narrow corridor curved in either direction. The air smelled much better here, Geordi thought, although it still seemed flat and metallic.

"Welcome to Neptune's Locker. That's what the people who work here call this undersea dome." Leilani's voice was almost an octave higher than it had been.

Lissa giggled at the change in Leilani's voice. The sound was high-pitched, like the voices in some old cartoons Geordi had once seen. Once started, Lissa couldn't stop. The laughter was contagious, and everyone but T'Varien joined her.

"I fail to see what you find so amusing." T'Varien's expression was faintly alarmed. "At this depth, the station must use a helium-oxygen atmosphere. This is to prevent people from becoming intoxicated from nitrogen in the bloodstream."

Geordi tried to stop laughing long enough to explain. "Everyone sounds so different." He started giggling again. Studying how helium altered sounds was completely different from hearing your own voice suddenly changed to soprano. He'd expected the change, but he couldn't help laughing at how silly he sounded.

"It's all right," Leilani said. "Everyone has the same reaction the first time. We maintain surface pressure and atmosphere in the shuttle as we come down. You don't have to worry about having 'rapture of the deep.' "

T'Varien pulled her eyebrows together in a look of fierce concentration. "What about the nitrogen we were breathing?"

Leilani's smile showed that she had been expecting the question. "That's why we keep the shuttle at surface pressure. Studies show the nitrogen is forced from your bloodstream within minutes because of the greater air pressure here in the station.

"When we return to the surface, we'll take about four times as long as we did coming down. That lets us gradually reduce the pressure in the shuttle's cabin. We'll also change the air mix back to surface normal as we go up."

T'Varien shook her head. "I still do not understand why everyone is laughing. It is not logical."

She really doesn't understand our humor, Geordi thought. It was hard to realize how differently Vulcans thought. He tried to control his laughter. "That's *why* we think it's funny. Because it *isn't* logical."

She shook her head, struggling with the idea. Geordi tried to find a better way to tell her why they were laughing. It wasn't easy. When you had to explain a joke, it wasn't as funny as when you heard it the first time.

Leilani glanced at her PADD. "We've got a full schedule this afternoon. If you're ready, we'll get started."

She started down the corridor. Geordi followed her, and the other cadets fell in with him. He couldn't wait to see what their next project would be.

* * *

Leilani led them along the corridor. It followed the outer rim of the station, curving ahead and behind them. Thick viewports, as dark as the ocean beyond, looked outward. Opposite them, sliding doors led to the interior of the station.

The inner walls of the corridor were flat fish tanks. Each section was filled with water, algae, and seaweed. The plants helped keep the station's air fresh and breathable. Geordi had read how the system worked with nature as much as possible.

Heavy pressure doors divided the station into sectors. When they passed the third set, Geordi paused to examine them. Sensors were located throughout the station to detect sudden changes in air pressure or to report water in the corridors. If the hull started leaking, the doors sealed off that sector. Control panels beside the door overrode the automatic systems. That let repairmen get to the damaged hull.

Halfway around the station, Leilani stopped. Painted across the door in dark blue letters was the sign: Science Department, Research 1. Leilani palmed the door's control pad.

"Why don't the doors just open for us?" Lissa asked. She gave the control pad a suspicious look as she passed it. "I feel like a criminal or something. We shouldn't have to *ask* to get in to the public areas."

Before Geordi could say anything, Yoshi spoke. "Underwater station has many doors, Honorable Lissa. Station keeps doors closed for safety. If hull leaks, water will not go past closed door."

"Thanks a bunch, Yoshi." Todd sounded tense.

That gave Geordi something to think about as they

followed Leilani deeper into the station. Starfleet cadets were the best and the strongest people in the Federation. In spite of that, he was edgy about this field trip and about being in such a dangerous place. His classmates also seemed worried.

Was there a reason they were nervous? Were they all sensing an impending disaster? Geordi snorted at his foolishness. It wasn't impossible that everyone would make the same psychic prediction, he supposed, but it was very, very unlikely.

That left only one explanation. Lieutenant Muldov had analyzed their psychological profiles. When he assigned their mission, he had chosen a field trip that played on their hidden fears.

That made sense to Geordi. Life in Starfleet meant dealing with the unknown. If you couldn't make your fears work for you, you'd never survive away-team duty. Proper respect and a healthy dose of fear would keep you alert on an unexplored world.

Figuring that out made Geordi feel better. He was used to dealing with alien worlds. His blindness, and later his VISOR, showed him a far different world than what the people around him saw. For his classmates, this field trip was the first time they had dealt with that strangeness. Most of them, it seemed, were finding the experience a little unsettling.

Nobody was born knowing how to handle alien environments. Even Starfleet cadets had to learn how to handle strange, and possibly hostile, situations. It was much better for them to learn that lesson now than to face it on an away-team mission where lives depended on their actions.

Geordi shook his head. How many lessons within lessons had Lieutenant Muldov put into this field trip? Clearly their grades would be based on much more than the reports they had been assigned to write.

Geordi almost ran into Yoshi when they stopped. Startled, he stepped back, running into Ven.

"Watch where you are going!" Reacting to the unexpected impact, Ven pushed Geordi away. For someone of his slight build, the Andorian was amazingly strong.

Geordi stumbled against the door frame. Somehow, he snagged his VISOR on a projecting edge and knocked it loose. He grabbed for it and settled it back into place, shaking. For a few seconds, he couldn't make any sense of the visual inputs.

He leaned against the wall, waiting for things to return to normal. He heard the door open, heard his classmates file past him into the lab.

"Are you all right?" Leilani put her hand on his shoulder.

Some of the tension left Geordi. He nodded. "My VISOR isn't supposed to come loose like that. But once in a while—" He shrugged. "I guess nothing's perfect."

Leilani felt along the door frame. "There's a bump here, right where it would catch your VISOR."

"That figures." He wiggled the VISOR against its contact points. "It feels a little loose, too. I wonder if the pressure or the atmosphere is affecting it."

"It's possible. Sometimes we have trouble with our equipment when it first comes down from the surface."

Geordi checked the VISOR again. "It's working fine now." *I'll just have to avoid walking into walls for the rest of the day,* he promised himself.

51

"In that case, let's join the others." Leilani grinned at him. "I think you'll like this part."

The room was small, barely large enough to hold the entire group. Counters were built into three of the room's four walls. Each work station held a helmet and control gloves, with monitor gauges and video screens on the wall.

A short, dark-haired woman was talking to someone through her communicator as Geordi entered. She had her back to the door. "That's right. We've got a student group here now. They'll be running Unit Five for the next hour."

"Got it," answered a voice from the ceiling. "We'll schedule the remote links for later this afternoon, then. Brooks, out."

The woman turned around slowly. She was wearing a gray worksuit and a metallic mesh vest that sparkled when she moved. Although she looked young, Geordi got the feeling she had worked here a long time.

"Welcome," she said with a smile. "I'm always pleased to see Starfleet's latest group of cadets."

Leilani moved to the front. "This is Dr. Cris Hall. She's director of the telepresence studies done here—"

"Please, nothing so formal. Just Cris." Cris smiled and waved off the rest of the introduction. Geordi wondered if this act was staged for every group that visited the lab. "Besides, we're just playing with the toys here."

Leilani smiled back. "It may be play, but these 'toys' are the Federation's most advanced exploration tools. They allow us to study environments where it would be impossible to send a human."

Cris laughed. "You're stealing my lecture. But if you

52

cadets don't learn anything else today, remember this. If your work doesn't seem like play, find something different. Life isn't long enough to spend years doing something you don't enjoy."

She faced each cadet squarely for a moment. Light sparkled off the plates of her vest. It reminded Geordi of something—something very familiar. He frowned. What did that vest remind him of?

Cris smiled again. "End of lecture. Everyone, choose a station and we'll get to work."

Geordi took the closest chair and examined his equipment. The gloves were easy. When he put them on, they transmitted his commands to a robot explorer somewhere on the ocean floor.

The helmet, though, was a problem. It relayed visual information from the robot's cameras to the user's eyes. When properly adjusted, the helmet let its wearer see what the robot saw as it moved across the ocean floor.

These helmets were standard issue. Geordi had tried to use them before. They wouldn't work with his VISOR.

With a sigh of frustration, he pushed the equipment away. There was nothing he could do with that helmet. He couldn't complete this part of the assignment, either.

Geordi slumped in his chair. It wasn't fair! The harder he tried, the more things went wrong. How was he going to pass this class if he couldn't do any of the field-trip projects?

To make matters worse, Ven was sitting beside him. Cris had started on the far side of the room and was working her way toward him, helping the cadets adjust their helmets.

Ven glanced toward Geordi. "On an away team, you would endanger everyone because you cannot use the equipment."

He can't use this model of helmet, either! Geordi realized. The helmets were solid and fitted tightly over the head. They had no openings for the Andorian's sensitive antennae. "How does *your* helmet fit?" Geordi asked. It was a cheap shot, but he was tired of Ven's comments.

Ven didn't answer. For a moment, Geordi was sorry he'd said anything. Attacking Ven wouldn't solve *his* problems. He wished he knew what he was supposed to do since he couldn't use the helmet.

Cris dropped a pair of helmets on the counter between them. "Why don't you two try these on?" she asked. "I think they'll work a little better than standard issue."

Geordi glanced at the helmets. Ven's had an open framework. He could adjust the supports to fit his head and, more importantly, to avoid his antennae. The other helmet didn't look any different from the one Geordi already had.

Ven grabbed his helmet and put it on. He swung the eyecups into place, adjusting them to fit. After tightening the straps, Ven slipped his hands into the control gloves. His fingers twitched as he picked up his robot and began exploring.

"What are you waiting for?" Cris asked with a trace of laughter in her voice. "I'll think you don't want to play with my toys."

"It's not that." Geordi turned the new helmet over in his hands. To his surprise, the internal wiring had been greatly altered. He wasn't sure what most of the new parts did.

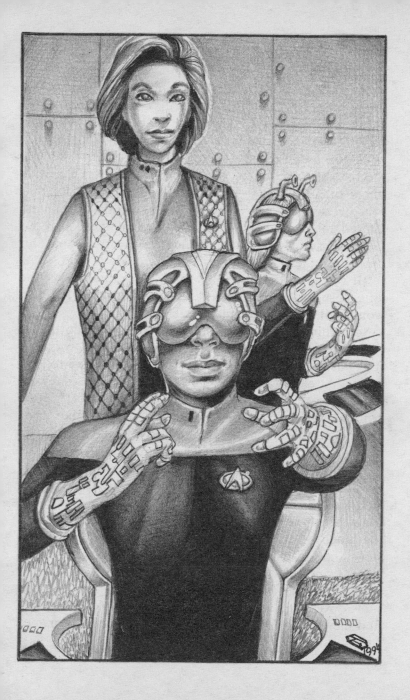

"It should work for you." Cris pointed to the contact points on either side of the helmet. "I had the Academy's Medical Officer send down the specifications for your VISOR. Having equipment you can use is your *right.*"

"I, uh, I don't know, that is, I—" Geordi examined the helmet to cover his confusion. Because of the wide range of humanoid body shapes and physical abilities, every Federation citizen could have essential equipment altered to his or her personal requirements. Somehow, Geordi hadn't expected Starfleet to worry about his unique problems until *after* he graduated.

"It was my pleasure," Cris said. "This finally gave me an excuse to see how they designed your VISOR. It's a wonderful piece of technology."

Something in her voice struck a chord in Geordi. He had heard his VISOR called many things, but "wonderful" was not a term most people used. He turned to look at her. At close range, the tiny sensors on her vest were impossible to miss. Like the facets of an insect's compound eye, each sensor picked up part of the scene around her. Computer implants fed the information to her optic nerves, bypassing her damaged retinas. This let her "see" her surroundings better than a sighted person.

Suddenly, Geordi remembered where he had heard of Cris Hall. Several years ago, while his parents were visiting the university on Olbrecht Five, terrorists bombed the biochemistry research facilities. The resulting explosions and fire filled the nearby buildings with dense, poisonous smoke.

Most of the scientists were overcome by chemical fumes. Rescuers, blinded by the thick smoke, could not find the victims. Without help, a graduate student named

Cris Hall pulled eight people from the marine biology lab before the rescue squad arrived. Geordi remembered the incident because, like him, Cris Hall was blind.

"You went to the university on Olbrecht Five." Geordi hadn't realized he was going to say it until the words popped out. "I remember hearing about what you did during the bombing."

"You heard about that? Small galaxy." She laughed. "That was a long time ago. Try your helmet."

Geordi removed his VISOR and put on the helmet. At first, he couldn't make the connections work. He adjusted the helmet several times before he got a solid contact. Even then, what he was seeing was nonsense.

After a moment, he realized the problem was the difference between the two devices. The VISOR presented him with a broad range of data that he then interpreted. The telepresence helmet was connected to a robot with limited senses. The robot's sensors reported the most useful information about an extremely alien world. He'd have to rethink what he saw through the helmet.

"Have fun." Cris squeezed his shoulder briefly. Her footsteps whispered against the tile floor, moving away from him.

He started to call her back, wanting to ask her more questions about the helmet. He didn't understand everything about how his VISOR worked. That made him doubly curious to learn how she had altered the helmet for him.

Before he could say anything, his brain *connected* with the information coming through the helmet. Suddenly, Geordi was in an alien world. He was clinging to the side of a cliff, looking down on the strangest sight he had ever seen.

CHAPTER
7

He was perched on a vertical sheet of cracked and broken rock. How the robot had gotten up the cliff, Geordi couldn't guess. He wasn't sure how to get it down, either. Even someone with lots of experience using remote equipment would have trouble getting out of this position.

Straight below him, rounded boulders and jagged blocks of dark rock littered the ocean floor. He turned his head, and a cone of light followed the movement. Anything situated more than a few feet away was blurred by the murky water.

The ground shivered beneath him. Pressure pulses, like waves passing, pushed against his right side. Curious, he looked in that direction.

At the edge of his vision, dense black "smoke" billowed from an irregular column of rock. Geordi struggled to see what was happening. Suddenly, as if he were zooming through the water, the boiling clouds jumped in front of him.

He tried to make out the details, but the light was too poor. Whether the robot's lenses were focused close or far, the light from his spotlight determined what Geordi saw. To get a better look, he had to get closer.

How was he going to get down the cliff? Geordi wondered. There were almost as many kinds of remotely operated robots as there were jobs for them to do. Nobody had said anything about what type of robot he was using. That meant either that he should already know how to run the robot or that the directions were readily available. Geordi decided the information must be somewhere in the computer. He just had to figure out where. If, like his classmates, he had used the helmets before, he would know the answer.

What was the correct command? "Computer" reached the main system on a starship or in certain areas of the Academy. It didn't work everywhere, though. Geordi chuckled, remembering a classmate who had asked for the answers during a test.

The computer in this station seemed much like a starship's. If he had designed the system, Geordi thought, he would have used a different command to access the robot's controls.

"Robot," he whispered into his microphone. Nothing happened, and his robot remained motionless. "Command" and "control" didn't work, either. He was starting to feel desperate. He'd never be able to face his classmates if he had to ask for the command.

"Remote?"

A menu in soft green letters appeared on the lower corner of his view. His left pinkie moved the cursor. He flipped through his choices. Everything he needed was there. Relieved, Geordi asked how to make the robot move.

It took several minutes to sort through the directions. His robot could do many different things. It was, he discovered, a high-powered research and exploration unit designed to work in dangerous environments. Rugged and durable, it could withstand years of hard work under harsh conditions. If Geordi wanted, he could drop the robot off the cliff without hurting it.

He could not, however, float himself free. For all its abilities, this robot was a walker, a ground-based unit. In an emergency, he could dump his samples and head for the surface—once. The robot would have to be serviced before it returned to the ocean's floor.

Geordi thought about taking the quick route down. What would happen, though, if the robot landed on its back? He looked, but that information wasn't in the manual. If he was lucky, he could get the robot turned over. But if he wasn't, he'd have to call for help.

That convinced him. He checked his equipment list, looking for another way down. After a moment, he found his answer—a tether line.

He searched the rock face for an anchor point. The grapples on his eight legs were firmly embedded in cracks in the rock, but those places wouldn't hold the line. He needed something he could tie it around.

Geordi went back to his equipment list. There had to be a way to anchor his line to the rock. After three times through, he was about to give up. Everything he found would leave him permanently fastened to this spot.

Then inspiration struck. The robot had a drill for taking rock samples. All he had to do was take a sample *through* the slab of rock. He ordered the robot to begin drilling.

The robot's side opened and a flexible arm snaked out. Geordi wiggled his fingers in the control gloves. He was surprised at how little effort it took to move the robot's arm. When he had the drill in position, he chose the "Go" command.

The arm went rigid and the high-speed drill bored into the rock. Through the helmet, he heard the whir and rasp of the bit. The sounds were much softer than if he had been there, but they still set his teeth on edge. The scene bobbed and jerked from the vibrations.

Much sooner than Geordi expected, the drill cut through the rock. Quickly, he turned the drill off. The arm pulled itself and the rock core back into its compartment.

Geordi considered throwing the rock sample away. After all, he hadn't chosen that spot because the rock was particularly interesting. The robot would travel faster if it wasn't carrying the extra weight. Still, how many of his classmates would collect rock samples at all? He might score a few extra points for bringing back a "typical" sample.

In the end, Geordi kept the rock. Maybe, if he collected enough information, he could make up the piloting points he had lost this morning. To go with his sample, he ordered the robot's computer to record continuous temperature and water-chemistry data.

It was time to get off the cliff. Geordi looped his tether line through the hole. Bringing the loose end around, he sealed the lock-it to the cable. It would hold until he released it.

Once he was sure the cable was anchored firmly, Geordi began working himself loose. One by one, he released the grapples and pulled the robot's legs against its body. Slowly, he paid out the tether line. The robot inched down the cliff.

At first it was easy. All Geordi had to do was pay out the line. If he went too fast, the robot swung into the cliff face. About halfway down, it started twisting as well. The combined motions made his head spin.

Geordi grabbed the side of the cliff with his robot. That didn't stop the scene in his helmet from swaying back and forth. The robot—and the rocks it was attached to—were still moving. An earthquake was shaking the sea floor.

What should he do now?

The earthquake lasted over a minute. Large rocks tumbled past him. The water slowed the falling boulders, but not enough. They could still damage the remote. Geordi kept his robot clamped to its perch, hoping nothing would hit it.

When things quit shaking around the robot, Geordi slumped back in his chair. He felt drained, almost as if he had been out there himself. "Computer, tell me about that earthquake."

"The earthquake registered 8.3 on the Richter scale," the computer said in his earphones. "It was centered one thousand kilometers north-northwest of this station and occurred five kilometers below the ocean floor."

Eight point three on the Richter scale? Geordi thought.

That was a major earthquake. No wonder his robot had bounced around so much. It must have been very close to the center of the quake.

He tipped the helmet away from one ear. The room was quiet except for the soft hum of the fans and the scritch of fingers moving on the counter. The other cadets, including Leilani, were calmly working their controls. As far as he could tell, no one else had felt the earthquake. His must be the only robot in that area.

Getting his bearings back, Geordi straightened his helmet. His robot was where he'd left it, halfway down the cliff. Off to his right, bigger clouds of black smoke poured out of the rock chimneys than before.

It isn't really *smoke,* he reminded himself. The streams of hot, chemical-laden water billowed and twisted like dense, black smoke from a major fire. The first scientists who saw the rock columns with their streams of metal-rich water had called them black smokers. The name stuck.

He looked for the best way to get close to the chimneys. With luck, he could sample them. He grinned to himself. The deep oceans were so remote and so hard to reach that every sample was important. Even after centuries of studying the black smokers, geologists were still learning how they worked.

First, Geordi had to get the robot off the cliff. He looked back along his tether line. When he released his holds, the robot would swing like a pendulum. That thought was enough to make his stomach do flip-flops.

Geordi buried the robot's grapples deeper into the rock. A pulse of current along the tether line released the lock-it. He reeled in the line, drilled another hole,

and tied off the tether. With the shorter line, he lowered himself to the bottom of the cliff.

Even then, it was rough going. The ground wasn't as level as it had looked from above. Boulders and rocks of many sizes were scattered everywhere. Narrow cracks and deep holes waited to swallow him.

He started off, picking his way through the obstacles. At first, it was very difficult. Geordi wasn't used to working with remotes. The control gloves were extremely sensitive, and they translated small twitches of his fingers into large motions of the robot's legs. It would have been much easier, he thought, if he'd gotten a floating robot.

After ten minutes, he got the hang of running the robot. It was a matter of practice, of repeating the commands until he didn't have to think about them. The robot's speed picked up. He was almost to the base of the nearest chimney.

The robot's spotlight showed Geordi a strange and fantastic sight. Hot water streamed through cracks in the sea floor. When it mixed with the cold ocean water, chemicals in the water formed tiny crystals of iron oxide and other minerals. There were so many of them that the water looked black.

As the crystals settled to the ocean floor, they made irregular mounds and knobby towers of rock. Patches of red and orange and black spotted the rocks. Feathery particles floated past the robot's "eye."

Geordi moved the robot around a low hill. On the other side, he stopped. Several dozen white clams grew beside a small crack in the ocean floor. To one side, a few short, stubby tubes clustered together. Eyeless worms lived in the tubes, and three of them were snapping at the water. He wondered what they were trying to catch.

It was too good a chance to miss. Geordi moved the robot nearer to the worms. He used his camera and sensors to record them from every angle, and he also took water samples from the crack.

I wish I could take one of the worms, too, he thought. However, his equipment list didn't have anything that would hold one. His robot wasn't built to collect living samples. The computer told him his samples wouldn't be retrieved for almost three weeks. That was when the service robot was due to visit this area.

He could still take rock and water samples. With a last look at the clams, Geordi returned to his original plan. There were so many interesting things to see in his area. His report would be the best ever written by a Starfleet cadet.

Geordi had been so busy observing the black smoker and collecting samples that he lost track of the time. Once he got used to the control gloves and helmet, the work was more like a game. *A game where the person who collects the most data wins,* Geordi thought. He was determined to win this time.

Suddenly, his world went black. The darkness was as complete and as shocking as if someone had yanked his VISOR off his face. At the same time, his seat vibrated like a shuttle fighting a high wind. It felt like a huge dog was shaking the station in its mouth.

"What's happening?"

"Earthquake!"

"Where are the lights?"

His classmates' questions mixed together and over-lapped. Geordi removed the helmet and fumbled for his VISOR. It wasn't where he'd left it. He reached farther, trying to find it.

It seemed like forever, but it was only a few seconds before his fingers closed around the familiar smoothness of the VISOR. It had bounced to the back of the counter. With relief, Geordi slid it over his eyes.

The room was still shaking. This was lasting a long time; even the biggest earthquakes didn't usually last more than a minute. He wished he had started counting immediately when it began. Now it was too late. He had no idea how long it had been since the earthquake started.

"Where are the lights?" Lissa asked.

"Aren't there any backup systems?" Todd demanded.

They were all sweating, and everyone but T'Varien was breathing in quick, shallow gasps. What they were experiencing was known as fight or flight response. Geordi wished he wasn't getting so much practical review for his Biology class.

At that, the flight portion of the fight or flight response sounded like a good idea. No one here would have time for a group of cadets after that earthquake. The scientists would be far too busy doing their work. Geordi wasn't as nervous as his classmates, but he was sure that was because he could still "see." He would have felt much differently if he hadn't found his VISOR.

The lights came on slowly, flickering and dimming. *Something is wrong,* Geordi thought. The emergency lights should have gone on immediately. Instead, the secondary, battery-powered system had taken over two minutes to begin working.

He looked for Cris to ask her what was happening. She wasn't there. That shouldn't surprise him, he supposed. They had been working with their remotes. There was no reason for her to be in the room all the time.

Leilani tapped her communicator. "Computer, report status of station." There was no response.

Geordi tried his communicator with no better luck. He frowned, trying to remember what he knew about space-station design. He was sure that the construction engineers had used similar ideas to build this undersea dome.

Most stations were made from separate modules. The computer and the power plant were in the central core. All the sections were linked by thick, flexible tubes that carried the electrical and computer cables. If the station's hull started leaking, the tubes could be sealed. Pressure doors, like the ones Geordi had examined earlier, closed off the corridors.

In theory, each section should be able to function independently in an emergency. They had battery power for lights and air circulation. Food and water weren't a problem, because rescue teams could reach them in less than six hours.

Geordi touched his rebreather again to reassure himself. Power and computer access had been cut off to their sector of the station, and he hoped that wasn't where the leak was. However, it *was* a possibility they had to consider.

A sharp jolt shook them. The floor heaved and tossed like a raft on a choppy sea. The walls groaned, protesting the motion.

The earthquake went on and on—thirty seconds, one minute, one minute and nineteen seconds. Even after it stopped, Geordi felt like he was still moving.

"I want out of here!" Lissa's voice cracked.

"I believe we should make our way to the shuttle." T'Varien sounded calm, but Geordi saw the telltale, jerky movements of her hands.

Leilani tried her communicator again, but there was still no response. "I don't like this," she said, frowning.

A siren wailed in the corridor. It held at full volume for over a minute. "Evacuation alert," a man's voice announced. "All personnel, proceed to the nearest docking port. This is not a drill."

"What do we do?" Lissa asked. "I don't know where *any* of the docking ports are."

"I do." Leilani's voice was firm. She radiated confidence, although Geordi could see that she was nervous, too. "I think T'Varien is right. We should return to our shuttle."

Leilani walked to the door and tapped the control pad. It didn't open. She waved her hand in front of the sensor. Nothing happened, even though the door should have opened. The safety systems were designed to get people *out* of damaged buildings.

Geordi examined the door. It wasn't a pressure door, which meant it wasn't holding them here because the corridor was flooded. His VISOR should detect the sensor beams controlling the door, but he couldn't see anything. The sensors weren't working. "We've got to find the override panel," he said.

The clones began poking at the wall. "In most civilian stations—" Amray said.

"—they hide the controls behind a plate—" Amril picked up the sentence.

"—usually about eye level on the left side."

Todd snorted. "Whose eye level? How do we know how tall the person was who installed those controls?"

"Oh! Of course!" That was the point, Geordi realized. Starfleet buildings were standardized. Knowing your way around one Starbase meant you knew your way around every Starbase. That made it easier for people to find things when they started a new assignment.

With civilian buildings, visitors didn't need to know where the access panels were. And Atlantis Station, in spite of the many Starfleet officers working there, was a civilian post.

Amril and Amray hadn't found the panel. Geordi crossed his fingers and guessed that it was high. His

VISOR gave him an advantage, but it wasn't helping much. Whoever had hidden the panel had done a thorough job.

He had almost given up when he saw a faint line on the wall. Then he knew why finding the controls had been so hard. The cover was shielded to hide the heat produced by the circuits.

Geordi was reaching for the panel when the floor began moving again. It shook harder and harder, throwing him off his feet. The emergency lights went out, plunging everything into blackness. The siren quit, its silence ominous and threatening.

The room tilted and lurched, tossing Geordi about. Gasps and groans, accompanied by dull thuds, came from his classmates. The station creaked, groaned, and shrieked. Beyond the door, plastic shattered and crashed on the floor. Water splashed against the wall.

We're doomed, Geordi thought. He waited for the water to pour under the door. Nothing happened, although the station continued to bounce.

Geordi pressed himself against the floor. He didn't want to get hurt now. He wasn't sure how they would get out of this mess, but he did know one thing—their chances were much better if they all could walk.

CHAPTER

Finally the station quit shaking. Geordi pushed himself slowly to his knees. The floor tilted, no longer level.

We're in big trouble, he thought. Sweat trickled off his forehead, but he was also shivering. He touched his rebreather, making sure he still had it. It looked like they would need their emergency equipment.

His classmates called to one another, asking who was hurt. Geordi ignored them. He was listening to the station noises. Each creak and groan had a story to tell.

He knew the station was very strong. It had to be, since it was in a dangerous and unstable environment. However, they had just been through three major earthquakes. How much more shaking could the station withstand?

"I want out of here," Lissa said.

"Everybody, stay calm," Leilani ordered. "The rescue teams will be here soon."

Geordi looked toward her. His VISOR showed him

her body temperature, and that told him she was lying. He looked for the others. Everyone seemed all right, except Ven.

He crawled to the Andorian. Ven was unconscious. Like the rest of them, he had been bumped around a lot. His antennae were mashed against his head.

Not broken, Geordi decided after checking them carefully. However, for Andorians, injuries to their antennae were serious. When he woke up, Ven was going to feel like the entire station had fallen on his head.

"Will someone look after Ven?" he asked. Amril and Amray were closest. They followed his voice to Ven's side.

"I do not think it is logical for us to remain here," T'Varien said. "Given the severity of the earthquakes we just experienced, I believe we should obey the evacuation order."

"Honorable T'Varien is correct." Yoshi sounded completely calm. "Samurai who does not save himself is unworthy to live."

"But we're trapped in here," Todd said. "We can't get the door open."

"I think I know where the switch is." Geordi crawled to the door. "I found the panel just before that last earthquake hit."

"Then get us out of here!"

Finding the panel was harder with the power off. Without the telltale heat readings, Geordi had to rely on his sense of touch. Even after it was opened he didn't know the circuit layouts, and he had to guess where the switch was. It took several tries to find it.

"I've got it," he said. "Are we ready to go?"

"We don't know what will happen out there." Lissa's voice shook. "This may be the only safe place on the station."

"She has a point," Todd said. "If we haven't been rescued, maybe this is the only intact sector."

"I don't think so," Geordi said. "But those earthquakes may have shaken the station loose from its moorings."

"Earthquakes of that magnitude often cause landslides." T'Varien sounded like she was thinking out loud. Geordi felt a moment's surprise that her ideas agreed with his. "The rocks beneath the station could have given way," she concluded.

"Then we'll fall to the bottom of the ocean and they'll never rescue us!" Lissa began crying. "Why did I ever want to live on a planet? Space stations are so much safer!"

Geordi struggled to keep from laughing. Billions of people still believed space was too dangerous a place for humanoids to live. Lissa's reaction put their situation into perspective.

"I think T'Varien is right," Leilani said. "However, the mooring cables are anchored into bedrock. We need to get to the shuttle before the cables break."

"What about everyone else?" Geordi asked. "Should we look for other survivors?"

"We have to go through the research areas to get to the shuttle," Leilani answered. "We'll look for others on our way out."

"What about the research that people have been doing?" T'Varien asked. "If the station is destroyed, all the records will be lost."

"Not everything." Leilani paused. "But a lot of to-day's reports will be lost. Most people store their backup records in the main computer on the island, but some don't update their files as often as they should."

Lose all that data? Geordi shuddered. The point of Atlantis Station's work was to learn how to predict earthquakes and volcanic eruptions. The earthquakes they had just been through showed how important that work was. They also proved that the scientists didn't have all the answers.

"Could we collect the data chips while we're searching the labs for people?" he asked. "We won't have time to get everything, but it's better than nothing."

"I'm not going to waste my time on a bunch of stupid data chips," Todd yelled. "I'm getting out of here!"

"You *are* going to collect those chips," Leilani ordered. "We all are. It takes five seconds to empty the main storage drawer. *If* you're far enough into the room to make sure there's no one inside."

"You can't make me waste my time on data chips! I won't do it."

"I rank you, Cadet Devereau. I will use the number of isolinear data chips you retrieve to decide whether you have checked the labs thoroughly for survivors. Is that clear?"

After a long pause, Todd answered, "Yes, sir!"

The others mumbled their agreement. Geordi didn't think anyone liked the idea. He, too, would prefer to run straight for their shuttle. However, they had a duty to rescue any injured people and as much of the station's data as they could.

"Are we ready?" Leilani asked. "Let's go."

Taking a deep breath, Geordi pulled the override. He hoped their guesses weren't too far off the mark. What dangers waited for them on the other side of the door?

The door crept open in short, unsteady jerks. Obviously, no one had tested the manual system since the station was built. Geordi held his breath, hoping the gears weren't too gummed up.

The door stopped halfway open, and he couldn't budge it further. He glanced at the others. For most of them, the narrow opening wasn't a problem. However Ven—who had regained consciousness—was still dizzy and confused. He leaned on Amril and Amray for support and they could barely keep him moving.

Geordi gave the door another shove, but nothing happened. If the other doors were in similar shape, they would have trouble rescuing either the scientists or their data. Either way, they couldn't stay here.

"Let's go," he said. He squeezed through the opening. While he waited for the others to join him, he tried his communicator. There was still no response. Either no one was in range or the station shielded his transmissions too well.

He looked around. A weak, battery-powered emergency light flickered at the end of the hall. The floor was littered with broken plastic from one of the fish tanks on the wall. The water and algae had splashed all over the floor, making it wet and slippery. Some of the dying plants gave off a faint greenish glow. Between that and the emergency lights, the others could see what they were doing. No other people were in sight.

Geordi picked up a piece of the plastic, fingering the sharp edge. His VISOR showed him the residual stress patterns in the material, but it didn't tell him which type of plastic it was. One of the newer ones, he guessed. They were often designed for specific jobs, especially in places where long exposure to metal was undesirable.

He couldn't think of any reason to keep the plastic, but it had a sharp edge. On impulse, he put it in his belt pack.

Amril and Amray helped Ven through the lab's door. They were the last ones out. The Andorian was very disoriented.

Leilani examined Ven. "I think he'll be all right," she said. "We don't have much choice about moving him."

"Like none," Todd said. "I'm not going to wait here with him for the medical rescue team."

"That is unworthy thought, Honorable Todd. One should protect fallen comrades so they may rise to continue fighting. True samurai have no fear of death." Yoshi seemed perfectly assured of his position.

Todd glared at him. "If it's all right with you, I'd rather get out of here before this thing falls off the mountainside."

As if to underline his words, the floor lurched sideways. The station bounced a couple of times, settling against its mooring cables. The walls groaned.

"Let's not argue," Leilani said. "Geordi, Todd, and Yoshi—check the labs on the left side of the hall. T'Varien, Lissa, and I will get the labs on the right side. Amril and Amray—get Ven to the shuttle. Move it!"

Geordi took the first door on his side of the corridor. A glowing red patch marked the emergency door release. He slapped the red spot, threw the cover aside, and pulled the lever. The door slid open easily.

He entered the room. The counters held an incredible framework of pipes, tanks, and equipment. Most of the tanks had fallen to the floor and shattered. A few were still in place, filled with bizarre-looking sea animals.

Farther into the room, Geordi stepped on something

soft. His foot slid out from under him, and he landed on his rear—hard.

It took a minute to catch his breath. Just beyond his foot was a palm-size white clam similar to the ones he had seen with his robot. He started to stand, and then he saw the body.

The scientist had been old. *Almost old enough to retire,* Geordi thought. He was very, very dead.

Fighting for control of his stomach, Geordi forced himself to his feet. With his head turned away from the body, he reached for the data storage rack. He dumped the data chips into his belt pouch and ran from the room.

Much to his relief, the next four labs he checked were empty. He circled through each room quickly, grabbed the data chips, and hurried out. The station hadn't moved again, but little creaks and groans reminded him that the structure could shift at any time.

The last lab held another body. Even though the woman was much closer to his own age, Geordi didn't react as much to her death. After making sure she was dead, he collected the data chips and left.

The others were standing beside the pressure door that led to the next section. As he approached, Geordi felt a sinking feeling in his stomach. What were they waiting for? He couldn't think of any *good* reason.

"The controls are jammed," T'Varien said. "I do not know the overrides for this model."

Geordi went up to the door. One glance at the telltales confirmed his worst fears. "It's not jammed. The controls are on security lockout." He turned and faced his classmates. "The next section is flooded."

CHAPTER

"We're trapped!" Lissa's voice shook. "I don't want to die here!"

T'Varien stared at her with blank incomprehension. "Hysteria is not logical. Your rebreather will provide sufficient oxygen until the rescue teams arrive."

Despite her level tone, T'Varien was shaking. Geordi thought she was almost as upset as Lissa. At least with T'Varien, Geordi could understand her reaction. Being surrounded by this much water must be affecting her. He could imagine her explanation: "Having so much water in one place is not logical."

Well, logical or not, they had to get through the flooded section. Waiting for the rescue team sounded less appealing by the minute. "Leilani," he asked, "is there any way around this section?"

She shook her head. "Not without going clear around the station's rim. Usually, we could go through the central core, but it's sealed off. That's why the computer is down and the main power is off."

"You can't be sure of that." Todd glared at Leilani. "You haven't checked."

"No, I haven't." Leilani shoved her hair away from her face. "But I know this station. It was built to take a lot of punishment. And the only time the computer links should disconnect is if the central core floods."

"You still don't know!" Todd insisted. "I vote we go through the central core."

Geordi thought about how long that would take. The earthquakes had shaken the station badly, and he didn't know how long they had before the structure failed. If one section was leaking, others probably were, too.

Leilani tapped her communicator. "Can anyone hear me? We're in Sector SR5A. Is anyone within communicator range?"

There was no answer. Leilani tried again, with no better results. "Either everyone made it to their escape pods, or—" she shrugged, leaving them to finish her thought—*we are the only people left alive in the station.*

Prying the cover off the control panel, Geordi examined the exposed circuits. He whistled. "Boy, is this ever an antique!" He remembered using such a board for a school science project. His fingers groped for the emergency battery.

"I can get the door open," he said. "But all that water will pour through here at once. We'll have to hang on to each other, or it will wash us away."

"It's too dangerous!" Todd started back the way they had come. After four steps, he turned to see who was following him.

Amril and Amray exchanged worried looks, glanced at Ven, and then looked at each other again. The Andorian was only partially aware of his surroundings. "We believe the shortest route—" Amray began.

"—is the one we should take." Amril finished the sentence.

"All roads are equal to true samurai," Yoshi said. Geordi wasn't sure what he meant, but he didn't follow Todd.

Lissa started toward Todd, then paused. No one else was going with her. She glanced from Todd to the others.

"It is not logical to assume that this is the only section that is flooded," T'Varien said in a small voice. "The earthquakes have been much more severe than this station was designed to withstand."

"That's it, then," Leilani said. "Geordi, what do you need us to do?"

Geordi looked at the telltales again. The pressure door was a pair of doors connected by a flexible tube. The tube let different sections of the station shift position relative to each other. This helped the structure weather severe earthquakes without breaking apart.

The gauge told Geordi only that there was water on the other side of this door. If the tube had ruptured, opening the door would flood this section without getting them into the next one.

He crossed his fingers and popped the battery out of its socket. "The control unit is off-line," he said. "We should be able to pull the door open now."

Leilani guided the Stenarios girls and Ven into the corner. "You two keep Ven back against the wall. Geordi, Yoshi, and Todd will pull open the door while the rest of us make sure they don't get washed away. Everyone, put on your rebreathers."

They opened their cases. Geordi fitted the lightweight plastic mask over his nose and mouth. When he pushed the seals against his face, the air-purifying unit on his waist started working. He checked the hose that went from the mask to the rebreather unit, making sure nothing leaked.

Finally, he examined the gauges to see that everything was working properly. The readouts were fine, but the model number was wrong. He rechecked it, fighting the cold feeling in his stomach. This style of rebreather was a light-duty unit, designed for use in shallow water. It had power for, at most, six hours of operation. They had that long to get back to their shuttle.

Should he mention the problem? Geordi wondered. After a moment, he decided to keep quiet. He should have plenty of time before his batteries ran out, and the group didn't need any more problems.

The other cadets were in their assigned places before Todd put on his mask. Reluctantly, he joined Geordi and Yoshi. The three boys worked their fingers into the narrow gap and pulled. Nothing happened. They tried again, with no better luck.

They changed positions before the third time. With some careful maneuvering, each found a spot to brace a foot against the door frame. They pulled, but still nothing happened.

"Are you sure you took the battery out?" Todd snarled. "Or did you lock it so we're stuck here forever?"

"I don't know. I'll look again." Geordi popped the

control panel out of its clips and turned it over. As he had thought, he'd removed the battery. So why was the door still locked?

He studied the circuit labels more carefully. The panel wasn't as familiar as he'd originally thought. One section was completely different, and several optical fibers linked those circuits to something deeper in the wall. *More backup systems?* he wondered.

There was one way to find out. Geordi took the piece of sharp plastic from his waist bag. With one stroke, he cut the fibers. "That's the best I can do," he said.

Todd scowled, but braced himself in the doorway. Geordi and Yoshi returned to their places. Once more, they pulled.

The door came open easily. Geordi stumbled backward, falling into T'Varien. She pushed him into the corner, then stopped, staring. A wall of water poured through the door.

Geordi grabbed her and pulled her against Ven and the clones. Yoshi and Lissa crowded against T'Varien, but Leilani was having trouble. Todd had been too far into the hallway, and the water had caught him.

Leilani wasn't strong enough to pull him back. Her feet were sliding on the wet floor. Soon she would lose her footing, and both she and Todd would be swept away.

What could he hold on to? Geordi looked around frantically. The only possibility was the opening where the control panel had been. He shoved his arm into the hole, grabbed a support beam, and wrapped his free arm around Leilani's waist.

With Geordi's help, Leilani swung Todd out of the

main current. Finally, Todd got his feet under him, and Leilani pulled him to the group. The cadets on the outside linked arms to keep everyone together.

The water pushed the door farther open. At first, the bigger opening didn't make much difference. There was too much water beyond. It smashed through the opening and thundered down the corridor.

Spray splattered Geordi's back, soaking him to the skin. The water level climbed quickly up his legs. It rose from his ankles to his knees to his waist within seconds.

Geordi shivered, wondering if he'd guessed wrong. What if it *was* the connecting tunnel that had the hole in it? Could they get into the next part of the station after this sector flooded?

The racing tide slowed to a strong river and, finally, to a lazy current. The water remained only waist deep, for which Geordi was grateful. This far down in the ocean, the temperature was barely above freezing. His feet and legs were growing numb from not moving. Leilani was shivering uncontrollably, and the other cadets looked equally miserable.

When he thought he could keep his balance, Geordi started toward the door. To be safe, he held on to the opening where the control panel had been. Cautiously, he looked through the door.

The tube was intact, but the other door was half-open. Something had jammed it, keeping it from closing all the way. The emergency light behind him was weak and flickering. It cast a pale yellow rectangle onto the flowing water. Geordi looked below the water's surface, swallowing hard when he saw what held the door open.

One of the scientists had tried to get through the door as it closed. He hadn't made it. To make matters worse, the door had caught his uniform. Between the door and the snagged uniform, the man had drowned before he could free himself.

Geordi released his grip on the panel and moved forward. Bracing his foot against the other door frame, he pulled against the door. To his surprise, it slid easily. He stumbled, almost losing his balance.

The scientist's uniform came free from the door's track. The body floated loose and drifted past Geordi. Behind it, carried along by the current, was more debris. Waterlogged clothing, unidentifiable personal objects, and two more bodies washed through the doors.

Geordi flattened himself between the doors to let the junk go through. The water was flowing at a fair pace. It wasn't so fast that they couldn't move against it, but they would have to be careful.

He looked up the corridor. Everything was dark and blurry, with the edges smeared together. Dismayed, Geordi realized there was barely enough light for his VISOR to detect. To make matters worse, the cold water was leaching the heat from the walls, the debris, and the bodies. Soon, everything would be the same temperature, and he wouldn't be able to see heat differences, either.

Then the significance of the current hit him. Water was still getting into the station. With this door open, it could now fill both sections. Considering the pressure at this depth, the leak had to be small. Otherwise the water would have refilled this section as fast as it poured through the door.

"Come on, everyone," he said. "Let's get out of here before the water gets any deeper."

"And before we freeze to death." Leilani's teeth chattered and she was shivering uncontrollably. "Link arms to keep together."

The cadets moved out of their huddle. The cold had revived Ven a little, and he watched his surroundings with greater awareness. He let the clones lead him, but he held onto their arms with enough strength to show them he knew what was happening.

In the waist-deep, icy water, they moved slowly. The current swept odd bits of clothing and assorted junk past them. It was a bad sign, Geordi thought. They were most of the way to the next pressure door, and they were still moving up current.

The sound hit them first. It was like the roar of a huge waterfall. Geordi thought it sounded as if millions of steel balls were being slammed into the water every second. With each step, the noise grew louder.

They came around the bend of the station. Where they should have seen the next set of pressure doors, a curtain of water stretched two-thirds of the way across the corridor.

"Oh-oh," he said. He could barely hear his own voice.

A seam between the hull plates had split. The water blasted through under high pressure. The entire width of the corridor seethed with foam. White froth splashed as high as the ceiling. Only the tremendous strength of the station's hull kept the roof from collapsing.

"What do we do now?" Lissa stared at the wall of water. "We can't go through there, can we?"

"We've got to go back." Todd straightened to his full height, trying to look like he was in command.

Still shivering, Leilani shook her head. "The shuttle is docked to the next section. With that much water coming through here, we don't have time to backtrack."

Geordi studied the wall of water, wishing he had a little more light. Even with his VISOR compensating for the low light levels, he was having trouble seeing details. And details were what he needed now.

He tried to remember what he had seen when they arrived. The leak was about ten feet from the door, he thought. That meant there was room for them to get to the door. No one could stand under the force of that water long enough to operate the door controls.

Just a little more light, he thought. *That's all I need.* He wanted to double-check his memory. Unfortunately, the only light source was too weak and too distant to do him much good.

Frustrated, Geordi stared at the shimmering wall of water. Did he have the right to risk his classmates' lives on an uncertain memory? How much time did they have before the rising water paralyzed them?

What should he do? It was the first life-or-death decision he had ever made. And if he didn't act soon, the cold water would decide for him.

Geordi looked at his fellow cadets, but no one offered him any answers. It came back to the same question: How well did he remember what he had seen earlier?

Before Geordi could decide, the floor began shaking. His first thought was that he was imagining things, that the cold had frozen his brain. However, waves rippled

Atlantis Station

the water in rhythm with the shaking. Geordi didn't think he could have invented that.

He splashed to the head of the line. "There's room on the other side." He had to shout to be heard. "Stay by the wall and don't let go of each other."

Desperately hoping he was right, Geordi started forward. Much to his surprise, everyone followed. The water felt heavy, viscous, resisting his movements.

The noise became deafening. *Before we get past this,* he thought, *my ears will be as numb as my feet.* In a way, he was glad he couldn't hear anything but the pounding water. Debating second thoughts wouldn't get them to safety. *All I can say is, I'd better be right.*

Near the leak, the spray drenched them. Icy mist soaked Geordi's uniform and plastered it to his skin. Streams of water ran down his face. His legs were numb and his teeth chattered. Leilani nodded her head as though she was falling asleep. That wasn't a good sign. Her brain was shutting down from the cold.

As they approached the wall of water, the current broke into violent eddies and whirlpools. The cross-currents tugged and pushed at him from all directions. It was almost impossible to keep his balance. Geordi pushed forward. They didn't have any choice.

He was two steps past the leak when his foot slipped. His legs were too cold for him to catch himself, and Geordi splashed into the freezing water.

In a panic, he struck out for the end wall. His arms still worked, but he couldn't feel his legs. The current pushed him toward the door. His outstretched hands touched the wall.

Shivering violently, Geordi dragged himself upright.

89

By the time he was standing, the others had joined him. Yoshi tried to say something, but the noise from the pounding water was too loud for Geordi to make out the words.

He looked around, congratulating himself that there was more room than he remembered. He waded to the door. To his surprise, it was open. He looked through the opening and shuddered.

Water shot through half a dozen pinhole leaks in the roof with enough force to cut metal. Something bumped into his legs. Geordi looked down, spotting the cover for the door's control panel.

"How far is it to the aquashuttle?" Geordi murmured. He tried to remember, but he felt so exhausted. It would be so good to take a nap, a nice long nap. When he woke up, he would be in his bunk at the Academy, warm and dry.

No! Panic shot through him. His body was dangerously chilled, and his brain was shutting down. He shook his head to clear it.

"We must get to shuttle quickly," Yoshi said.

The cold made it difficult for Geordi to see. With the emergency lights out, he was using residual heat. However, his VISOR couldn't separate things that were the same temperature. The images were dim and fuzzy, and becoming dimmer all the time.

"We could use flashlight now," Yoshi said, echoing Geordi's thoughts. He wished they had brought one of the shuttle's high-powered waterproof flashlights with them.

"It is illogical to wish for that which we do not have," T'Varien said.

"Well, here goes—" Geordi started forward, picking a snakelike path around the water jets. That added to the time it took to get to the shuttle, but they didn't have much choice. They were all very tired and thoroughly chilled. An accident right now—any accident—would be extremely dangerous.

Finally, Geordi saw the tunnel leading to the docking port. They had almost made it! A ragged cheer went up from the others when he pointed to the door.

Geordi picked up the speed a little, although it was impossible to hurry in the cold water. Still, just a few meters away lay warmth and safety and, if they were lucky, dry clothes.

The floor began to shake. Geordi was too tired and too cold to be sure, but he thought this earthquake was a lot stronger than any of the previous ones.

The water jets widened and the thunder of the water grew louder. Over the pounding, roaring water, the station's structure creaked and groaned. Something ripped in the wall nearest him.

"Jump!" Yoshi yelled.

Geordi threw himself across the hall. Broken plastic and chunks of paneling sprayed the area where he had been standing. In slow motion, the wall separating the corridor from a storage room disintegrated. Beams, panels, and chunks of conduit rained into the water.

Shaking from the cold, Geordi pulled himself to his feet. One by one, the other cadets surfaced. Everyone seemed a little dazed.

Todd had a long gash on his shoulder. It was bleeding freely, and Geordi felt dizzy from seeing so much blood. He was glad Lissa volunteered to help Todd.

Leilani floated to the surface and hung there, motionless. Geordi wondered if she had hit her head, but he couldn't find any damage. Finally, he decided she had surrendered to the cold. If they couldn't revive her soon, she would die.

He tried to lift her from the water, but her limp body was too heavy for him. T'Varien stumbled to his side, her movements stiff from being too long in the frigid water. The two of them dragged Leilani upright. T'Varien checked the seals on her rebreather mask. They were secure, but the gauges on the waist unit had all changed to amber.

"These units are rated for six hours," T'Varien said. "It is not possible for the batteries to be running low already."

Geordi checked the model numbers on the girls' rebreathers and glanced at his own unit. His battery light showed a warning amber color. T'Varien's did, too. "They're shallow-water units. They don't work well in cold water. We've got maybe fifteen minutes of power left," he said.

Amray grabbed his arm and pointed toward the fallen wall. "My sister."

Geordi counted heads. Amril and Ven were not there. He looked where Amray was pointing. Beneath the collapsed wall were two blurred patches of warmth. The missing cadets were trapped under the wreckage.

CHAPTER 10

"I see them," Geordi said. "That chunk of wall landed on them."

"Are you certain that they are under there?" T'Varien asked.

Geordi tapped his VISOR. "I see the heat from their bodies."

"Are they hurt?" Amray asked.

"I can't tell. We'll have to get them out first." Geordi looked to see who could help. Todd and Leilani were in no shape to do anything, and Lissa was still binding Todd's wound. That left Yoshi, T'Varien, and Amray to help him.

He looked at Amray. "If we lift the wall, can you pull them out?"

"Yes." Her tone said she would do anything to rescue Amril.

They waded to the collapsed wall. "Mass of wall does not look too large," Yoshi said.

"However, its surface area will create a considerable amount of water resistance." T'Varien tilted her head to one side, as if calculating the exact numbers.

Geordi nodded. "Something that big will be awfully awkward to handle in the water. Also, there's all that heavy junk on top of it."

They started to work. Geordi and T'Varien moved the heaviest beams, while Yoshi and Amray cleared away the other debris. It took almost five minutes. Geordi tried not to think how long the batteries in their re-breathers would last. Leilani, and now Ven and Amril, were alive because they were wearing their masks. As tired and as cold as everyone was, any fall could be fatal without them.

Geordi stared at the panel, trying to decide where exactly Amril and Ven were. The eddies in the cold water and the thick insulation on the panel made it difficult for him to tell. Even when he used the VISOR at its maximum sensitivity, all he saw were vague smears of warmth.

"Can you specify where they are trapped?" T'Varien asked.

Geordi stepped to the side, trying to see things from a different angle. They had been standing near the wall when the earthquake hit. Most of the cadets had made flat, shallow dives that carried them across the corridor. From what he could see, Amril and Ven had not moved.

"They're here," he said, sketching the location with his hands. "Let's try to get them out from this side."

T'Varien and Yoshi nodded. They moved beside him and squatted, working their fingers under the panel's edge. Amray crouched at his side, waiting.

"One, two, three," Geordi counted. They heaved upward. It was like dragging a large plate through molasses.

Geordi gritted his teeth and pulled harder. The muscles in his thighs protested. Slowly, the panel lifted. Ten centimeters, twenty, thirty. It was much harder work than he had thought it would be.

Finally, Amray squeezed into the opening. She wiggled forward on her stomach. Ven was closest. Amray grabbed his arm and crawled backward, dragging him after her.

Ven was unconscious. When Amray released him, he floated to the surface, limp as a rag. Even without going to him, Geordi saw the amber warning lights on his rebreather. His batteries were almost exhausted, too.

"We'd better hurry," he told the others. He seemed short of breath. Was it his imagination, or was he running out of air?

Yoshi squatted down, putting his shoulder under the edge of the panel. Seeing how much more leverage that gave him, Geordi copied him. T'Varien shifted position, too.

"Now!" Yoshi said. All three straightened their legs. Geordi felt his boots slipping, but he kept pushing. The panel moved another fifteen centimeters upward.

Amray crawled between them. The extra distance was enough to free Amril, and Amray pulled her clone sister free. Amril was shaken, but with Amray's help, she climbed to her feet.

Once the clones were clear, Geordi braced his hands against the panel's bottom edge and stepped back. T'Varien and Yoshi copied him, holding the panel at

95

arm's length. They looked at each other, and Geordi
nodded.

"On the count of three," he said. "One, two, three."
They released the panel. It settled into the water,
sending out a wave that almost pushed Geordi off his
feet. *Not that it would take much,* he thought. He was
just about done in.

"Let's go," he said. He and Yoshi each took one of
Ven's arms, dragging the unconscious Andorian through
the water. After a worried glance at her sister, Amray
went to help T'Varien with Leilani. Amril followed
Amray closely, her movements slow and uncertain.
Geordi wondered if she'd been hurt by the collapsing
wall, but he didn't see any obvious injury.

Lissa put her arm around Todd's waist and led him
forward. He seemed out of touch with his surroundings.
Geordi figured he was in shock from his wound, but they
couldn't do anything until they reached the shuttle.

The ten meters to the connecting corridor were the
longest of Geordi's life. No one had much to say. They
were all too tired and cold to spend their energy on
anything but dragging themselves to safety.

He was dizzy with relief when they reached the pressure door. With all the practice he'd been getting, it took
him only a minute to disable the door's controls. The
door slid open, revealing the dry stretch of corridor that
led to their shuttle.

The water poured through the opening. This time,
rather than waiting for the current to slow, the cadets
let the water push them through. Geordi grabbed onto
the door, swung himself through the current, and ducked
behind the door. The others tumbled through after him.

Fumbling for the latch with his cold-stiffened fingers, Geordi popped the cover off the door's manual controls. They had to close it before the water flooded the corridor. He threw his weight against the lever.

The water was a living force, clawing and smashing its way through the opening. Slowly, the door started to choke off the flood of water. Yoshi stumbled over to Geordi and added his weight to the effort. Together, they forced the door shut.

Geordi slumped against the wall, leaning on the lever and panting for breath. Yoshi flashed him a tired, happy grin. They had gotten the door closed in time. There were only a few centimeters of water on the corridor floor.

After he got his breath, Geordi started to get up. When he took his weight off the lever, it moved upward. The door slid back, letting in a stream of water.

Yoshi looked from the door to the lever, frowning. The corridor walls were bare, with no tool lockers or equipment racks. With a shrug, Yoshi stumbled over to Ven. Removing one of the Andorian's boots, he brought it back and jammed it behind the lever.

Slowly, Geordi released his grip. The lever squeaked against the boot, compressing the material. For a moment, he was afraid it wouldn't work. The lever squeezed the boot until it caught against the hard material of the sole. Geordi heaved a sigh of relief. The door would stay closed. They could walk through the nice, dry corridor to their shuttle.

The fourteen meters from the door to the shuttle felt more like four. Geordi was so relieved to see their ship that the distance evaporated, even though he was helping

Yoshi carry Ven. They reached the shuttle, opened its door, and stumbled in.

Geordi eased Ven to the floor and headed forward, pulling off his rebreather. Through the front viewport, the water was black. When the power was up and running, he'd turn on the searchlights and take a look at the station. Sliding into the pilot's seat, he closed the shuttle's door and set the heater to maximum. He didn't know how hot it would get, but at the moment, high noon at midsummer on Vulcan's Forge sounded just about right. As the heat began to flow into the shuttle, he leaned back in the chair and surrendered to his exhaustion. When his brain thawed out, he'd decide what to do next.

He was starting to feel pleasantly warm, despite his wet clothes, when someone put a hand on his shoulder. "We found some towels in back." Lissa handed him one. "Unfortunately, there aren't any spare clothes, but T'Varien thinks she can make some hot soup from the stuff in the ration packs."

"Thanks." Geordi straightened, suddenly feeling a whole lot better. Drying off and getting something to eat were exactly what he needed. He went to work with the towel, squeezing the water from his uniform. It was amazing how much better he felt. With the heat set on high, it wouldn't take long for his uniform to finish drying.

The clones searched through the storage lockers and located the other supplies. Geordi took two of the candy bars they offered and nibbled on them while he checked out the shuttle's systems.

Behind him, the others were toweling off, too. Lissa

had appointed herself head nurse and was putting a field dressing on Todd's shoulder. Leilani and Ven, both barely conscious, were wrapped in blankets from one of the storage lockers. *This whole crew needs a stay in Sickbay,* Geordi thought.

He powered up the shuttle's systems, preparing for departure. If he hadn't been afraid that the earthquakes had damaged the ship, he would have skipped all the routine checks. The computer was probably still keeping score on their piloting, but he didn't care. Right now, a fast escape was a higher priority than a good grade, so he raced through the systems check.

"Strap down," he called over his shoulder, satisfied that they were ready to leave.

"All set," came the answer from half a dozen overlapping voices.

Geordi crossed his fingers and disengaged the grapples. He waited for the reassuring *chunk* of the clamps falling away from the airlock, but there was only silence. Geordi repeated the command, but still nothing happened.

He stared at his status board, wondering what to do. The sensors said the clamps had been released. The other possibility wasn't something he wanted to consider.

Cautiously, he engaged the starboard thrusters. The shuttle didn't move. He applied more power, but they remained where they were. The shuttle was still attached to the station. Geordi powered down the thrusters. They would have to manually release the grapples from outside the ship.

Before he could unfasten his safety harness, the shuttle began shaking. *Not another earthquake,* he thought. The shuttle jerked back and forth, like a short, stubby tail attached to the body of the station. The readings of the shuttle's depth gauge were changing, too, showing deeper and deeper water around them. Neptune's Locker was headed for the ocean depths, still anchored to the rocks where it had been built.

CHAPTER

11

"What's going on?" Lissa asked. A low growl, like the roar of a cargo shuttle's engine, built up behind them.

"Landslide." Geordi had to shout. "We're going along for the ride." The aquashuttle bounced, tossing Geordi against his safety harness. The shuttle's headlights traced drunken arcs through the water, showing him first a blurred jumble of rocks and dirt, then an empty expanse of cold water.

"What does Honorable Geordi propose to do?" Yoshi asked. "Has surface station dispatched rescue squads?"

"I don't know." Geordi reached for the call button. It took three tries to hit it. An empty hiss answered him, punctuated by the crackle of interference from the station's automatic data relays. They were on their own.

A loud crash sounded from outside and below them. The shuttle dropped sharply, then rebounded and traced a half circle through the water. A large chunk of bulkhead pinwheeled past them, tumbling end over end into the darkness. They landed hard, jerked sideways, and bounced again. The shuttle's frame groaned, protesting the abuse. Rocks and debris clanged against the shuttle's hull, almost deafening Geordi with their noise.

He gripped the sides of his seat, holding on while the shuttle slammed into the sea floor and recoiled four more times. How much abuse could the little ship take? It was well designed and ruggedly built, but he didn't know any design criteria which covered this situation.

"When we stop moving, I'm going outside." One at a time, he wiped his palms on his legs. *You don't have time for the jitters now!* he told himself. "The grapples wouldn't let go."

"That is dangerous undertaking," Yoshi replied. The shuttle jerked sideways, throwing them against their restraints. Yoshi gasped for breath. "I, too, will go. Perhaps with more muscle, job will be done quicker."

"Thanks, Yoshi." Geordi was surprised at how much better Yoshi's offer made him feel. Too many things could go wrong once he left the safety of the ship.

"I, too, will go," T'Varien said. "There are three skinsuits in the locker. Logic dictates that we employ all available resources to free ourselves."

Geordi looked out the window. More chunks of debris sailed past them, but the shuttle appeared to be moving slower. He glanced at their speed gauge, which confirmed his guess. "We're slowing down. Let's suit up so we'll be ready when we stop."

T'Varien handed the suits forward. Geordi unrolled his, admiring the lightweight, waterproof fabric that was also pressure-resistant. The suit even had self-sealing boots and gloves. The bright orange, reflective material

103

was easy to see, even in low light. Geordi smiled, thinking he would almost enjoy going outside wearing this suit. If only the situation weren't so dangerous—

It took some effort to get into the suit. He didn't want to unfasten his safety harness, so he had to twist and squirm in his seat to get his arms into the sleeves. The continued movement of the shuttle didn't make things any easier. Although they were still slowing, each bounce came at the wrong time. Geordi was sure he would be bruised all over from slamming into the safety harness and the side of the shuttle's control panel.

He looked out the window and froze, his hands clenched. Two rock towers, twenty-five or thirty meters high and as many meters apart, loomed out of the darkness. The shuttle—and the station—was headed straight for them. "Brace yourselves!" he yelled. "We're going to crash!"

Geordi leaned over and tucked, his arms wrapped over his neck. The shuttle slewed to one side, throwing him against his harness. Then, with a terrifying shriek of protesting metal and a deafening crunch, he was tossed around in his seat.

The shuttle vibrated from the impact. When he realized they were no longer moving, Geordi lifted his head. Behind him, he heard the sounds of the other cadets as they sorted themselves out. "Is everyone okay?" he called.

The answers were a little ragged and shaky, but everyone was unhurt. "What happened, Honorable Geordi?" Yoshi asked.

"I think we hit something." Geordi looked out the front, but saw only empty water. "I can't see anything from here, but we were headed for a couple of nasty-looking rock fingers."

"It would be logical for us to proceed with maximum speed to accomplish our mission," T'Varien said. She was pulling on her boots as she spoke.

"Good idea." Geordi released his harness and slid his feet into his boots. He moved to the back, surprised at how shaky his legs felt. After all the bumping and bouncing they had been through, his body hadn't adjusted to their stationary position.

T'Varien and Yoshi were waiting for him, already dressed. Yoshi handed Geordi a metal crowbar, a utility belt with a rebreather unit, and a helmet.

"There are three sets of grapples," T'Varien said. "The most efficient plan is for each of us to take one."

"Agreed." Geordi strapped on the utility belt, settled the helmet over his head, and connected it to the rebreather unit. When he lifted the crowbar, he felt ready for anything.

T'Varien removed the emergency hatch. The small, round opening was protected by a force field that kept the water out of the shuttle while allowing divers to pass through. Geordi stepped through the hole. T'Varien and Yoshi followed him.

Geordi clipped his safety line to an anchoring pad. Without waiting, he started up and over the shuttle. He'd decided to take the far set of grapples.

Swimming in the skinsuit was much nicer than wading through the station in his uniform. The skinsuit held in his body heat. He could swim for several hours before becoming dangerously chilled, even at this depth. If not for their danger, swimming in the deep ocean would have been fun. After the noise and confusion of the last few hours, it was quiet and peaceful outside the ship.

From the top of the shuttle, he got his first good look at their position. The station was caught between the two rock spires which reminded Geordi of the black smokers he had explored with his robot. By sheer luck, the shuttle was between the spires, hanging over a steep slope that vanished into darkness. The last sideways jerk had kept them from being crushed against the rocky towers.

Geordi drew in a nervous breath. The station's position didn't look stable. He thought about how hard they had hit and wondered how long it would be before the station's weight would break the spires. When it slid over the edge, the station would land on the shuttle and crush it.

He looked toward the station and shivered. Large gaps in the dome's structure marked where hull panels had been wrenched loose. Beams, metal plates, and miscellaneous equipment were strewn across the ocean floor. He saw two emergency airlocks, both without their escape pods. Geordi hoped that meant that some of the scientists had escaped from the station.

"Enough sight-seeing," he muttered to himself. He pushed off against the hull. When he reached the airlock, he caught the grapple to stop himself. The two large metal claws were still firmly closed around the shuttle's docking rings. The claws looked normal, except they should have been open.

Taking the waterproof torch from his utility belt, Geordi played the bright light over the grapple. At first, everything seemed normal. Geordi started over, looking more carefully, and at last found the problem. The grapple's claws were twisted just enough to keep them from opening.

He slid the crowbar between the claws and braced his feet against the shuttle. To his surprise, his first pull moved the claws over a centimeter. Encouraged, he tried again.

It took him five minutes of prying with all his strength, then stopping to catch his breath. The grapples were designed to hold ships twice the size of the aquashuttle, and the claws on each grapple were almost as big as Geordi himself. Even so, most of their holding power came from the magnetic fields, which he had deactivated. It had taken a lot of force to jam the grapples.

Finally, the clamp opened with a shriek that set his teeth on edge. Geordi pushed the claws away from the rings. *Now to see how the others are doing,* he thought.

T'Varien was just pushing the claws on her grapple away from the docking rings as Geordi touched down beside her. A tremor shook the metal surface beneath his boots.

"What was that?" Both of them mouthed the words at the same time. A pulse of water shoved against Geordi's shoulder.

Is the station breaking loose? he wondered. He looked at T'Varien and realized she was thinking the same thing. They pushed off, swooping around the airlock to join Yoshi.

The third grapple was so badly bent that one person couldn't budge it. In the time Geordi and T'Varien had opened the others, Yoshi had barely gotten his crowbar between the claws of this grapple.

Geordi and T'Varien anchored themselves beside him. Using all his strength, Geordi couldn't get his crowbar into the opening. T'Varien wiggled the tip of hers into the narrow line and threw her full Vulcan strength against it. The line spread, and she jammed her bar deeper into the gap.

Geordi planted his crowbar beside T'Varien's and forced it downward. Yoshi leaned against his crowbar and pulled. Even with their combined strength, it was slow work. One centimeter at a time, the claws spread.

Another tremor shook the shuttle, stronger than the last. A feeling of panic swept over Geordi. They weren't going to make it in time!

Desperation lent him strength. He threw his entire weight onto his crowbar. A shriek of metal scraping against metal rewarded him. The claws separated and dropped away from the docking rings.

Yoshi pushed off, shooting toward the hatch like an orange porpoise. T'Varien was slower and a lot less graceful. Geordi trailed behind, giving them time to go through the hatch.

Halfway around the shuttle, a pressure wave caught him. Before he could regain his momentum, another pulse hit. In slow motion, one of the rock spires toppled over and vanished. Behind him, the station skidded closer to the edge.

Geordi activated his belt winch. It reeled in his safety line, hauling him through the water. He pointed his hands ahead of him, trying to minimize the resistance and maximize his speed. Nothing could stop the station from going over the edge now. They had very little time to get the shuttle free.

109

When he got to the emergency hatch, T'Varien was waiting. She dragged him through the opening. Geordi raced for the cockpit while Yoshi closed the hatch.

Another tremor rocked the shuttle. Geordi threw himself into the pilot's seat and powered up the engines. This time, the thrusters pushed them away from the station.

Violent currents tossed the shuttle about. Geordi fought to keep the unpredictable water movement from slamming them into the sea floor. On the viewscreen, the station skidded to the edge, balanced for a moment, and then fell, pinwheeling onto its roof. It slid out of sight, gathering speed.

More pressure waves buffeted the shuttle. Geordi fought to hold the ship steady until the water calmed. Then, finally, he flipped the shuttle and pointed it toward the surface.

He engaged the autopilot, setting it to warn him if they encountered anything unusual. After confirming their heading, he headed aft to take off his skinsuit and get some hot soup.

CHAPTER 12

The trip to the surface took several hours. As they rose, the computer slowly reduced the cabin pressure and changed their air to surface normal. After all their adventures, they didn't need to get the bends by coming up too fast.

For most of the time, Geordi dozed in the pilot's seat. The autopilot was doing its job, but he was afraid something might go wrong. He called the surface station several times during the first hour, but the empty hiss of static was the only response. Finally, he gave up. Either something was blocking the signals or the station's communications were out.

It was after midnight, local time, when the shuttle reached the ocean's surface. Geordi looked out over the moonlit water, thinking he had never been so glad to see anything. Then he caught his first sight of Isla del Fuego. He tapped his VISOR, checking to see that he was receiving its signals correctly.

"Oh, wow!" Lissa swung herself into the copilot's seat and stared out the front window.

Isla del Fuego was living up to its name. The volcano was in full eruption, with streams of red lava snaking down its sides. Clouds of steam billowed upward where the molten rock entered the ocean. The bright moonlight turned them shades of pearl and silver.

Geordi tried again to reach the surface station. As he expected, no one answered. The station had either been evacuated or destroyed by the lava. He switched to the general Starfleet frequency and tried to raise the Academy. To his surprise, Lieutenant Muldov answered.

"It's about time you reported in, Cadet La Forge. Complete your assignment and return to base immediately. Muldov, out."

"What did he mean by that?" Lissa asked. A puzzled frown wrinkled her forehead.

"Beats me." Geordi felt as confused as Lissa looked. Their assignment had carried no instructions that covered this possibility. He guessed that Lieutenant Muldov meant they should gather as much data as possible before returning.

Their voices woke the others. The cadets clustered around the window. Geordi took the shuttle in closer to give them a better view and to record the scene with their scanners. He didn't get *too* close, though. After all their adventures, he wasn't going to risk anything happening to the shuttle.

"It would seem that the intense earthquakes have triggered a full-scale eruption," T'Varien said. "It is a most spectacular sight."

"That's for sure." Geordi grinned. Seeing the volcano erupt *almost* made up for the rest of their trip.

"Someday perhaps we will know enough to predict precisely when such eruptions will occur." T'Varien paused. "The evidence that suggested this eruption might occur allowed too many interpretations. Leilani said even the scientists on the station were split into two groups on the subject."

"Really?" It was nice to know the experts didn't know everything, even though he wished they'd been more accurate with their predictions this time. "I guess it's good to know there'll be some work left for us after we graduate."

Finally, everyone had seen enough and Geordi didn't think anything new was happening. He ordered the shuttle to take them back to the Academy. He was so tired

113

that he could barely find the controls, and only the thought of his own bed kept him going.

He had hoped they could slip in quietly, but that didn't happen. Half the senior staff was waiting to debrief them. He envied Ven, Todd, Amril, and Leilani. The medical officer whisked them off to Sickbay, leaving the others to answer the questions.

It was nearly dawn before the debriefing was over. "You cadets did very well," Lieutenant Muldov said. "Your efforts in retrieving the lower station's data chips will be commended. With the upper station buried by the eruption, it will be some time before we gain access to the data in those computers.

"Your group will have an extra day to turn in your reports for this assignment. Dismissed."

The five cadets started for their quarters. Geordi felt very pleased with himself. He and his classmates had gotten out of Neptune's Locker with no permanent injuries to any of them. They had been very lucky.

All the people on Isla del Fuego had been evacuated in time, although seven of the scientists working in the undersea dome had not made it to their escape pods. The Starfleet cadets, unfamiliar with the dome's layout, could easily have become additional casualties.

Geordi touched his belt pouch. Cris Hall had sent him a brief message congratulating him on his escape from Neptune's Locker. He smiled, thinking how relieved he'd felt to know she was alive. He was sure that was why she'd sent him the message.

The route to their quarters led past Sickbay. "I want to see how my sister is doing," Amray said.

The group decided to come with her. Todd and Leilani were asleep, but Ven was awake and asked to talk to Geordi.

"I owe you an apology, Geordi," the Andorian said. "My world is very harsh, and only the strongest survive. Anyone who is born less than perfect is abandoned at birth because they cannot compete in our society."

"Uh—yeah?" Geordi scuffed his toe against the floor, trying to figure out Ven's meaning. If the other cadets understood, they didn't give him any help.

Ven seemed embarrassed, as though apologies didn't come easily for him. "What I am trying to say is that I am grateful that you saved my life. I will remember this

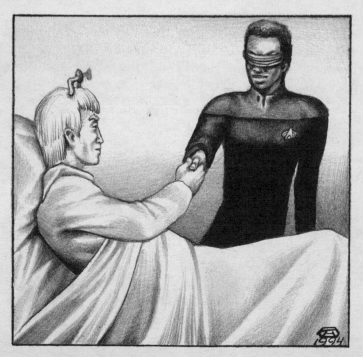

in the future when I am tempted to judge others by the customs of my planet."

A grin spread across Geordi's face. Similar grins lit the other humans' faces, and even T'Varien's expression showed a hint of warmth. Geordi reached out a hand to the Andorian. "Maybe we can teach each other about our people."

"I would like that very much." Ven clasped Geordi's hand. The two cadets, from very different worlds, smiled at each other across a gap that wasn't as wide as it had been before.

About the Author

V. E. (VICKI) MITCHELL has written two adult *Star Trek* novels—*Enemy Unseen* and *Windows on a Lost World*—and one *Star Trek: The Next Generation* novel, *Imbalance.* She has also had short stories and articles about writing published in a variety of places. When she isn't writing fiction, she works as a geologist for the Idaho Geological Survey, where her geological publications far exceed her fiction credits. Her hobbies include making costumes, dancing, photography, Chinese cooking, putting on science fiction conventions, and working on her Ph.D. She is married and is "owned" by a 125-pound black Labrador/St. Bernard whose main goal in life is to keep her working at her computer.

About the Illustrator

TODD CAMERON HAMILTON is a self-taught artist who has resided all his life in Chicago, Illinois. He has been a professional illustrator for the past ten years, specializing in fantasy, science fiction, and horror. Todd is the president of the Association of Science Fiction and Fantasy Artists. His original works grace many private and corporate collections. He has co-authored two novels and several short stories. When not drawing, painting, or writing, his interests include metalsmithing, puppetry, and teaching.